BREAM
GIVES ME
HICCUPS

BREAM GIVES ME HICCUPS

& other stories

JESSE EISENBERG

GROVE PRESS
NEW YORK

Printed in the United States of America
FIRST EDITION

ISBN 978-0-8021-2404-3
eISBN 978-0-8021-9081-9

Grove Press
an imprint of Grove Atlantic
154 West 14th Street
New York, NY 10011

Distributed by Publishers Group West
groveatlantic.com

15 16 17 18 10 9 8 7 6 5 4 3 2 1

CONTENTS

Contents

III. HISTORY

IV. MY ROOMMATE STOLE MY RAMEN: LETTERS FROM A FRUSTRATED FRESHMAN

V. DATING

VI. SPORTS

Contents

VII. SELF-HELP

VIII. LANGUAGE

IX. WE ONLY HAVE TIME FOR ONE MORE

BREAM
GIVES ME
HICCUPS

I.

BREAM GIVES ME HICCUPS

RESTAURANT REVIEWS

FROM A PRIVILEGED

NINE-YEAR-OLD

SUSHI NOZAWA

Last night, Mom took me to Sushi Nozawa, near Matt's house. Except she didn't let Matt come with us and I had to leave in the middle of my favorite show because Mom said we would be late for our reservation and that I didn't know who she had to blow on to get the reservation.

At the front of Sushi Nozawa is a mean woman. When I asked Mom why the woman is so angry, Mom said it's because she's Japanese and that it's cultural. The woman at school who serves lunch is also mean but she is not Japanese. Maybe it's just serving food that makes people angry.

Sushi Nozawa does not have any menus, which Mom said made it fancy. The Sushi chef is very serious and he stands behind a counter and serves the people whatever he wants. He is also mean.

The first thing they brought us was a rolled-up wet wash-cloth, which I unrolled and put on my lap because Mom always said that the first thing I have to do in a nice restaurant is put the napkin in my lap. But this napkin was hot and wet and made me feel like I peed my pants. Mom got angry and asked me if I was stupid.

The mean woman then brought a little bowl of mashed-up red fish bodies in a brown sauce and said that it was tuna fish, which I guess was a lie because it didn't taste like tuna and made me want to puke right there at the table. But Mom said that I had to eat it because Sushi Nozawa was "famous for their tuna." At school, there is a kid named Billy who everyone secretly calls Billy the Bully and who puts toothpaste on the teacher's chair before she comes into the classroom. He is also famous.

Mom said they have eggs so I asked for two eggs, but when the mean woman brought them, they didn't look like eggs; they looked like dirty sponges and I spit it out on the table in front of Mom, who slammed her hands on the table and made the plates rattle and so I got scared and spit out more sponge on Mom's hands and Mom yelled at me in a weird whispery voice, saying that the only reason she took me to the restaurant is so that Dad would pay for it. Then I started crying and little bits of the gross egg came out of my nose with snot and Mom started laughing in a nice way and gave me a hug and told me to be more quiet.

The mean woman brought me and Mom little plates of more gross fish bodies on rice. I asked Mom to take off the fish part so I could eat the rice. Mom said, "Great, more for me," and ate my fish. I like rice because Mom said it's like Japanese bread but it has no crusts, which is good for me because I don't eat crusts anyway. I also like it when Mom says "Great, more for me" because it seems like that is her happiest expression.

When the woman brought the bill, Mom smiled at her and said thank you, which was a lie, because Mom hates when people bring her the bill. When Mom and Dad were married, Mom would always pretend like she was going to pay, and when Dad took the bill, which he always did, she said more lies like, "Are you sure? Okay, wow, thanks, honey." Now that Dad doesn't eat with us anymore, maybe I should pretend to take the bill from Mom and say a lie like, "Oh, really? Okay, thanks, Mom," but I don't because lies are for adults who are sad in their lives.

The mean woman took the bill back without saying thank you. I guess she is not sad. But she is definitely angry.

I understand why the people who work here are so angry. I guess it's like working at a gas station, but instead of cars, they have to fill up people. And people eat slowly and talk about their stupid lives at the table and make each other laugh, but when the waiters come by, the people at the table stop laughing and become quiet like they don't want to let anyone else know about their great jokes. And if the waiters talk about their own lives, they're not allowed to talk about how bad it is, only how good it is, like, "I'm doing great, how are you?" And if they say something truthful like, "I'm doing terrible, I'm a waiter here," they will probably get fired and then they will be even worse. So it's probably always a good idea to talk about things happily. But sometimes that's impossible. That's why I'm giving Sushi Nozawa 16 out of 2000 stars.

MASGOUF

Last night, Mom took me to a new restaurant called Masgouf. Mom said that it was an Iraqi restaurant and that we had to go because we are open-minded people and we should support it. I thought it was weird though because Matt's brother is in the army in the real Iraq and their car says SUPPORT THE TROOPS. So it kind of felt like we were supporting the restaurant instead of Matt's brother.

Mom said that all the women in her book club already went to the restaurant, but I didn't know why that meant we had to go to the restaurant too. And I don't know why Mom is even in the book club, because she doesn't read any of the books and, on the nights before the book club meetings at our house, she says "fuck" a lot and asks me to look on Wikipedia. Then I have to read the plot synopsis and major characters to her while she vacuums, which is hard because the vacuum is really loud and I have to follow her around the house holding my computer and reading.

The first weird thing I noticed when I walked into Masgouf is that a lot of the people eating there were wearing big black face masks so you can only see their eyes. Mom said to me kind of disappointedly that she was hoping there would be more people who "look like us." But I said that we don't know what those people look like because they're hiding in the masks. Then Mom elbowed me in the neck, which is what she does when I say things that are either too loud or too quiet or if I'm laughing.

When Mom looked at the menu she said, kind of quietly under her breath, "Figures, it's fucking dry." I'm not sure what she meant by that but I think it has something to do with alcohol, because whenever Mom opens a menu, the first thing she does is look at the alcohol and breathe a sigh of relief.

Mom said that she would order for both of us and that we should share, which she usually says when she doesn't think the food will be good. When the woman came over to take the order, Mom looked at her like she was kind of a homeless person and said, "And where are you from?" When the woman said, "Iraq," Mom said, "Oh, beautiful, what city?" Then the woman said, "Baghdad," and Mom said, "Aww," as though the woman was crying, but the woman wasn't crying, she was smiling. So I looked up at the woman and I smiled very big to show her that I was not always on Mom's side, but when the woman saw me smiling she made a weird face like I was making fun of her, which I wasn't. Then Mom kicked me under the table and my leg hurt for the rest of the night and a little bit the next morning, which is today.

The first thing the woman brought us was a weird pile of rice on a plate and a big bowl of soupy-looking eggplant in a red sauce. I could tell Mom got a little nauseous by it but she smiled at the woman and said, "Wow. Traditional! Can't wait to dig in!" But I could tell that Mom was lying because when the woman walked away, Mom took a little bite of it, just with the front of her teeth, and then flared her nostrils like she wanted to puke right there at the table. Then she said, "Sweetie, I think you'll like this. Why don't you try it," so I knew she must not have liked it. Then Mom poured the eggplant stuff onto the rice and kind of moved it around the plate to make it look like we had eaten it.

Then the woman brought us the other dish, which was a chicken shish kabob with French fries. The French fries just tasted like French fries, even though they didn't have ketchup, and the chicken shish kabob just tasted like regular chicken. When Mom and I tasted how normal it was, we looked at each other in a relieved way, like we were Matt's brother and we had just come back from Iraq.

On the way home, Mom called all the women in her book club to tell them that we went to Masgouf. She lied the whole time, telling them how nice it was to spend some alone time with me and how interesting it was to see all the Iraq people in their black face masks, and that she didn't even think about Dad's new girlfriend one time during the fun and tasty dinner. When Mom lies, she doesn't just say things she doesn't mean, she says the *opposite* of the things she *does* mean. And probably most children would be angry at their moms for lying so much, but for some reason it just makes me feel sad for her.

When we got home I read Mom the plot synopsis for *Wuthering Heights* while she vacuumed in her underwear. Then Mom said her stomach kind of hurt and I thought that mine did too. So Mom and I both went to separate bathrooms and didn't come out for a long time. That's why I'm giving Masgouf 129 out of 2000 stars.

THE WHISKEY BLUE BAR
AT THE W HOTEL

Last night, Mom took me to a bar called the Whiskey Blue Bar, which sounds like a fun blue place but is actually a scary dark place where drunk people wear lots of makeup and pretend like they're happy by talking loudly.

Mom had a date with a guy she called her "Widower Friend." "Widower" means your wife died and "Friend," when Mom says it about a man, means someone rich who Mom is trying to marry. I never get to go on dates with Mom, but Mom wanted me to meet her Widower Friend because she wanted to show him what a good mom she can be to his two daughters, who no longer have a mother.

The Widower Friend didn't know I was coming when he asked to meet Mom at the Whiskey Blue Bar, and since I am not old enough to go to a bar, Mom said that we had to pretend to be staying at the W Hotel. I told Mom that I didn't want to lie to the hotel people, but Mom said it was okay in this case because it was just a white lie, which I guess is a lie that white people are allowed to say without feeling guilty.

Since Mom wanted to show the man how good she was with children, I knew she would be nice to me the whole night, and when the man walked in, Mom put her arm around me, which felt strange because she never does that and I never noticed how cold and bony her hands are.

When we all sat down, the man said, "Didn't know you'd be taking your son here." And Mom squeezed my shoulder again and said, "I just can't bear to be away from this guy. I love kids." I knew that Mom was going to lie about liking children but I thought she would probably think of a more creative way to do it.

The waitress came to our table and knelt down in a weird way like she wanted to show us her breasts. She was wearing a short black skirt and was really beautiful, except up close. She said, "What can I get you folks tonight?"

Mom said that she wanted a Strawberry Mojito and asked the Widower Friend in a kind of babyish voice, "Is that totally girly of me?" The Widower Friend smiled and blushed in a way that made me think he would have preferred to actually be on a date with a young girl instead of an old woman doing a baby voice. Then the Widower ordered his drink in a really serious voice, like it was important to get all the details right: "Dry Tanq Martini. Twist of lemon. Stirred. Don't bruise the gin." The waitress nodded very seriously and I suddenly thought that it was so strange to have a place that just makes drinks. Since they only sell one thing, they have to take it very seriously, and I guess no one ever tells them that what they're doing is not an important job.

Then the waitress showed me her breasts and asked, "And what can I get for you, little man?" Mom asked the waitress to make me a Shirley Temple, which I didn't want because it's named after a dead little girl named Shirley, but I decided not to say anything. Then Mom said, "Mix it weak, he's driving tonight." And the three adults laughed even though Mom's joke was a lie and also not funny.

When the drinks came, Mom finished hers kind of too quickly and ordered another one. The man sipped his slowly, which meant he probably didn't like Mom, and I just tried to fish out the cherry from the bottom of my drink because I was hungry.

The more Mom drank, the more she asked about the Widower's wife. I could tell that he didn't want to talk about his wife because he would change the subject, but Mom said weird things like, "Did Debbie ever try Cedars-Sinai Hospital? Because my friend Joyce is an amazing endocrinologist over there." I think Mom just wanted to show the man that she had a friend who was an important doctor, but because the wife had already died it seemed like a weird thing to say. The man seemed a little surprised, and I thought that maybe he was trying not to cry, and then he said kind of quietly, "We never tried Cedars-Sinai."

Normally Mom would be embarrassed for saying something so dumb, but because she was drunk, she didn't realize that she made the man upset. So instead of apologizing, Mom said, "I've been friends with Joyce since college. She's brilliant. And actually very well-read." The man just nodded.

Mom said she had to go "freshen up," which meant she had to go poop because alcohol makes Mom poop, and she left me alone with the guy. It was a little strange to be alone with him because I think he didn't really like that I was on his date. And then I couldn't stop thinking about his dead wife either and I just tried to not say anything about it, but I got so nervous that I said, "I'm sorry that your wife died from cancer." I knew it was the wrong thing to say but I couldn't get it off my mind and sometimes accidents happen even with talking. He said, "Thanks." And then Mom came back and I could tell that she must have pooped a lot because her face seemed relaxed.

When Mom sat down she said, "Ready for round three, Mr. Mister?" which meant she wanted to drink more alcohol with the man, but I could tell that the man just wanted to go home. I also wanted to go home but I knew that Mom wanted to stay so I didn't say anything. But the man looked at his watch and said something like, "I'd love to stay, but the girls are probably up worrying about me," which seems like something a normal parent would say, especially since his girls don't have a mom. This made me like the Widower Friend.

The man walked us to our car and gave Mom a hug, which Mom kind of held for a long time even though the man tried to pull away.

On the way home, I could tell that Mom was upset with the date and that maybe she thought it was partly my fault. I could also tell that Mom was drunk because she was driving all over the highway and we almost got into an accident with a man who rolled down his window and yelled at Mom in Spanish. Then Mom yelled something mean about Mexican people and I started to cry because the man kept yelling and it scared me even though I couldn't understand the words he was saying. Sometimes the things that are scariest are the ones you don't understand. That's why I'm giving the Whiskey Blue Bar 136 out of 2000 stars.

TCBY

Last night, Mom let me choose a restaurant and I chose TCBY, which stands for The Country's Best Yogurt. I know you're not supposed to brag and it's wrong to say that you have the best yogurt in the country, but Mom always says if you want something hard enough, you can get it. And since TCBY wants to have the best yogurt so much that they made it their name, maybe they do have the best yogurt.

Mom also let me take a friend and I chose Matt, who now likes to be called Matthew. Mom always calls Matthew my "little friend," which seems strange because Matthew's taller than me. He's also taller than Mom and I think she doesn't like him, but I think that's just because Matthew and I have a good friendship and Mom doesn't have any real friendships and Dad hates her and he said so in front of me two separate times before he left.

When I asked if we could pick up Matthew on the way to TCBY, Mom sighed loudly and said, "It would be easier for everyone involved if he just met us there." I thought it was a strange thing to say because the only people involved were us and Matthew and he lives on the way to TCBY. But I didn't argue and Matthew rode his bike and met us in the parking lot.

When Mom and I saw Matthew, he ran up to us and gave us both a hug, which is something Matthew has started doing a lot. I like it because I like when people hug me, but Mom kind of pulled back because she's not used to people touching her because no one ever does.

TCBY has a lot of flavor options, which makes me think they're really trying hard to be the best. I wanted Mom and Matthew to think that I made a good choice in going to TCBY so I said, "Wow, look at how many different flavors they have," and then Mom said in a sarcastic voice, "Thou doth protest too much, TCBY!" and Matthew and I looked at each other like we were trying not to laugh because what Mom said made no sense.

Matthew ordered a Mountain Blackberry Yogurt. He said that he got it because it's the most interesting color, which is a kind of light purple, but which Matthew called "mauve." "Mauve" is a word I never heard before and hearing new words is one of the reasons I like Matthew. When I asked why he didn't get the flavor he liked the most, he said he thought that all the flavors probably tasted the same and so it was best to get something that was "pretty to look at." Mom rolled her eyes two times: when Matthew said "mauve" and when Matthew said "pretty to look at."

The woman behind the counter asked Matthew what he wanted for toppings and he said Blueberries and Cherries. And then the woman said, "You just want two fruits?" Then Mom said, "Yup! Two fruits for my two little fruits!" And then Mom laughed in a cackling way that made everyone uncomfortable. When Mom finally stopped laughing, she said, "Sorry, I just couldn't help myself," and then we felt uncomfortable again.

When the woman asked me what I wanted, I decided to get the same thing as Matthew because he thought about his order in such an interesting way.

Mom ordered a cup of Dutch Chocolate Yogurt and asked if the chocolate was really shipped in from the Netherlands. The girl said she didn't know but that she could check. Then Mom told her not to bother and said that she'd get a cup of Dutch Chocolate because it's "so decadent." But I could tell by the way that Mom asked about the Netherlands and how she said "so decadent" that she was making fun of TCBY for being not fancy, but the girl behind the counter didn't know Mom's sense of humor so she said something real like, "It's one of our classic flavors." And Mom said, "Oh, it sounds like a *real classic.*"

When the woman asked if Mom wanted toppings, Mom said, "Oh boy! Where to begin? What does your sommelier think of the Butterfinger Pieces?" But since the woman didn't realize Mom was making fun of TCBY, she said, "Butterfinger Pieces are really popular." Mom said, "Oh, I'll bet," and laughed again.

Then Matthew and I looked at each other in a secret way because we thought it was weird how two people could have the same conversation but one of them is making fun of it and the other one is taking it seriously. It also made me feel bad for the TCBY woman because she didn't know she was being made fun of by Mom, which is sadder than someone who does know they're being made fun of because at least those people can fight back.

After a few bites of the Mountain Blackberry Yogurt, I got brain freeze and it hurt really bad. Mom said that brain freeze is not a real thing and that I should stop complaining, but Matthew told me to relax and to put my tongue to the roof of my mouth and lick. He demonstrated by showing me his tongue licking the roof of his mouth and then he put my head back and told me to open my mouth. But when I opened my mouth with my head back, Mom got really frantic and said, "Jesus Christ, you two, get a room!"

Mom ate a few bites of her yogurt, which had a lot of Butterfinger Pieces on it, but I could tell that she didn't like it, which I kind of expected because she ordered almost all of it sarcastically. At first I felt bad for Mom that she was eating something she didn't like, but then I realized that Mom could have gotten what me and Matthew got, which was delicious and pretty to look at. Instead, she chose to be mean and that's why she got something disgusting.

In a way, Matthew is a lot like TCBY. A few weeks ago, right after he changed his name from Matt to Matthew, he started calling me his best friend. I thought it was strange at first because I didn't consider him my best friend. I liked Todd and Cara as much as I liked Matthew. But the more Matthew *called* me his best friend the more I actually *felt* like his best friend and the more I liked him and the less I liked Todd and Cara. So I guess Matthew is like TCBY because they both said they were the best at something even before the other person agreed. I know it sounds like Matthew and TCBY are trying to have relationships in reverse, but I like to think of everything happening together at the same time.

Mom is the opposite of Matthew and TCBY. She never says that she's a good mother. In fact, every time she talks about being a mother, she says excuses like, "Lord knows I wouldn't win mother of the year," or "God knows I've made my share of mistakes." But TCBY says they're the country's best yogurt and Matthew says he's my best friend, and I guess, in a way, it forces them to try harder to be the best. But Mom never says she's the best mother so maybe she doesn't feel any pressure to be one. Maybe she actually feels pressure to *lose* mother of the year or make even *more* mistakes.

All I know is that I really like Mountain Blackberry Yogurt with Blueberries and Cherries and I really like Matthew. And Mom is angry and divorced from Dad and she doesn't like Dutch Chocolate with Butterfinger Pieces even though, out of all the options, that's the one she chose.

I know that I want to be more like Matthew and TCBY because when you say you're good at something it makes you try harder to be better and when you say you're bad at something it makes you try harder to be worse. That's why I'm giving TCBY 1954 out of 2000 stars.

ROBERT FROST
ELEMENTARY SCHOOL CAFETERIA

A weird thing happened at school today that the adults were really proud of but that the students thought was stupid. I don't have a total opinion yet but I think it's probably somewhere in between.

Our school was chosen to be part of a new program called "Healthy Lunches, Healthy Choices." In this program, famous chefs make school lunches that are supposed to be healthy but also good tasting. I know these things sound like opposites but the school is trying to say that they could be the same thing.

The principal called an assembly before lunch and congratulated us, which seemed strange because we didn't do anything except go to the school that got chosen by Healthy Lunches, Healthy Choices. The principal was standing next to a chef, who was smiling really big, and there were photographers taking pictures, and whenever the photographers moved, the chef would kind of turn his head so he was always facing them.

The principal said that we were part of a food revolution and that we were so lucky to have this famous chef personally cook us our first new meal. But we didn't feel lucky because no one cared about the chef or the principal or even about eating lunch. We just do it because it's in the schedule.

Normally the school serves usual school food like spaghetti and meatballs or fish sticks or pizza on Fridays. But I never eat that stuff because it's usually the same weird texture even though it's different food and it's put on a tray by a mean woman with a hairnet who scares me and also chews gum with her mouth open.

I eat the same thing every day: a chocolate-chocolate chip muffin, which means the cake is chocolate and there are also chocolate chips. I know it doesn't sound like a muffin is enough food, but they're not the normal-size muffins. They're really big and really soft except the top part, which has a crusty edge that's delicious and is chewy like gum, but a kind you're allowed to swallow.

For drinking, I always get a Snapple, which is actually a lemon Snapple, but lemon is the basic flavor so I just say Snapple and they give me a lemon one. I eat and drink the same thing every day because it makes me feel less nervous to know that it's there.

Sometimes, if Mom can't sleep because she's panicked about her life decisions, she'll stay up all night and pack me a lunch to distract herself from her bad thoughts.

But Mom's lunches are never actually possible to eat. One time, she packed me a single stick of Juicy Fruit gum, a box of toothpicks, and a note asking me to stay late after school because a gentleman friend was coming over. Today she packed me butter, a box of dry macaroni and cheese, and a book of matches. I think she just empties the refrigerator at night and takes the stuff she doesn't want and puts it in the trash, the garbage disposal, or my lunch bag.

Anyway, today's lunch by the famous chef was a few different things and I wrote them down so I would remember all the names of the foods, which I hadn't really seen before and which I would not really like to see again because they were gross.

The first thing was called "Arugula Salad with Roasted Beetroots." This was like a salad, but instead of lettuce and tomatoes, there were bitter leaves that made us all want to puke right there at our tables and beets, which are dark red balls that kind of look like bloody feces and which I have recently discovered produces just that.

The second thing was called "Poached Salmon with Dill." The salmon tasted like when you chew on paper and the dill part tasted like cut grass from the garbage of a lawn mower got caught in my teeth.

And the dessert wasn't really dessert. It was something called "Compote," which is really just another word for jelly that's hot and soupy, like throw-up made from Arugula and Beetroot Salad.

While we ate the gross food, the chef came around to our tables with a photographer. He put his arms around us and smiled for the pictures and said dumb things like, "Look out diabetes! Here comes a spoonful of compote!" or "I think I see a salmon swimming upstream with a delivery of omega-3s! Next stop, brain development!" He didn't even realize that we hated his food and, in a way, we hated him and hated that he ruined our day and maybe lunch forever.

Even if the food was really good, which it wasn't, the school shouldn't have made us eat it right away. They should have done it little by little, like putting a small amount of the dill stuff on pizza if they really needed to. I understand that they think they're being good by trying to make us more healthy, but it just seemed like they were so proud to have the chef there that they didn't think about what we would have wanted.

It's like just because the adults thought it was a great idea, we would too. But kids think differently than adults think. Adults have spent so many years thinking more and more like each other because the more you live with other people the less you think like yourself and the more you think like them. But kids are new people so we still think more normally. That's why I'm giving Robert Frost Elementary School and Healthy Lunches, Healthy Choices 256 out of 2000 stars.

ORGANIX VS. THE SAN GENNARO STREET FESTIVAL

Last night Mom and I went to two very different eating places: an organic restaurant and a street fair. And even though these places were very different, each one made me think about the other one in a new way, which is why I am writing about them together.

The first place we went to is called Organix and it is an organic and vegan restaurant, which is kind of like going to the doctor for dinner. On the sign outside, under the name Organix, are the words "Helping the Earth Grow," which makes no sense because the Earth is not getting any bigger, which is something I learned a long time ago and I'm nine.

When they give you the menu at Organix, they also give you a little booklet called *The Organix Bible*, which I guess is named after the real Bible, which is the story of Jesus Christ and God. *The Organix Bible* has a few pages, and while Mom pretended to read it, I actually did read it.

The Organix Bible was just kind of bragging about how great Organix was by saying things like, "At Organix, we off-set our light footprint in Mother Earth's beautiful skin by composting all organic material." And I thought that maybe it was a good thing to recycle, but saying things like "Mother Earth's beautiful skin" seemed kind of stupid and like it was written by a weird child.

Mom pretended like she was happy with the food, even though it was all disgusting raw vegetables, and acted like she normally eats this way because when the waiter asked if everything was good, Mom smiled and said, "Yes, I love the dressing, what is it?" And the guy said, "Aloe," and then Mom said, "I thought so! That's normally what we eat at home." And the guy said, "Yeah, it really soothes your digestive tract and warms the lumen." But I could tell Mom didn't know what he was talking about because she said, "And I think I recently read something about cancer." And the guy just kind of nodded because there was no real way to respond to what Mom said.

When the guy asked if we wanted dessert, Mom lied and said, "I'd love to see a menu." The guy said there was no dessert menu but that "Tonight's dessert is apples." That made me and Mom laugh a little bit and Mom said, "Just apples?" And the guy explained that the apples were special and from the other side of the country. And he seemed so proud of his apples that I felt bad for laughing, but Mom didn't feel bad and she kept laughing as she said, "We'll just take the check."

I guess I feel bad for people more quickly than Mom does and that is one difference I've noticed about us.

The first thing Mom said when we left Organix was: "Somebody bring me a hamburger!" But I didn't know who she was talking to and I'm not allowed to go food shopping alone.

As we were walking back to the car, we passed the San Gennaro Street Festival, which Mom said is "a party that Italian people have outside every year so the city can clean up their mess." The food smelled so good though, especially after being in Organix, which smelled like a bathroom that just got cleaned. When I asked Mom if we could get something to eat from the street fair, she said that all the food was disgusting. I said that the food at Organix was disgusting too, and Mom agreed but said at least the food at Organix wouldn't kill us like the San Genarro food.

I asked Mom for zeppoles, which are fried balls of dough with powdered sugar. Zeppoles are the kind of food that is really good while you're eating it but that makes you feel disgusting right after. I guess that's why the San Gennaro Street Festival can only happen once a year.

Mom said no to the zeppoles but said, "I think we've earned a cannoli." I asked her how we "earned" it and she said, "After ingesting aloe, I deserve a side of beef and a birthday cake." It's weird how Mom thinks that eating something you don't like is the same thing as hard work.

In our search for a cannoli, we passed four cannoli stands and each one had a different sign:

The sign on the first cannoli stand said, THE CITY'S BEST CANNOLI.

The sign on the second cannoli stand said, OLDEST CAN-NOLI RECIPE.

The sign on the third cannoli stand said, WORLD'S BEST CANNOLI!!!

The fourth cannoli stand did not have any sign. It just had a glass window to show the cannolis, which looked like all the other cannolis.

Mom said, in a low and serious voice, "Okay, mister. Which one should we get?" like it was an important test. I said that I thought they were probably all the same and that it didn't matter, but Mom said we had to find the best one.

Since there was no way to figure out which cannoli was the best, we had to use the signs to tell us which one to get. I thought very hard about this. And I started thinking that each sign maybe attracts a different kind of person and maybe you could actually tell a little about a person from the cannoli that they choose. For example, maybe someone who really likes New York would get a cannoli from the stand that says, THE CITY'S BEST CANNOLI, and maybe someone who was old or a chef would get one from the stand that says, OLDEST CAN-NOLI RECIPE.

But I decided that I wanted to get a cannoli from the stand with no sign because I was thinking that, by not having a sign, the stand was not trying to prove anything to me, and I liked them the most. And, in a way, the thing I didn't like about Organix was the same thing I didn't like about the signs: the more they told me how great they were and how much they were helping the Earth, the less I wanted to believe it.

I said, "I want to get a cannoli from the stand with no

sign," but Mom marched up to the WORLD'S BEST!!! stand and got two cannolis. When I asked her why she chose the WORLD'S BEST!!! stand, she said, "It's the world's best cannoli! That means there can't be any better cannoli. In the world! Think about it!"

But I did think about it. And I think that Mom was wrong. Just because someone says something doesn't mean it's true. And I think that the more someone says something, the less it's probably going to be true. That's why I'm giving Organix 147 out of 2000 stars and the San Gennaro Street Festival WORLD'S BEST CANNOLI!!! stand 162 out of 2000 stars.

THANKSGIVING WITH VEGANS

Last night, Mom and I went to Thanksgiving dinner at a Vegan family's house, which is kind of like going to temple for Christmas. Mom said that Vegans are "people who don't eat any meat or cheese or shave," and since Mom doesn't like to cook, she decided that we needed to go to our neighbors' house for Thanksgiving.

Thanksgiving used to be my favorite holiday because Mom and Dad and I would drive up to Dad's parents' house and Dad and I would roll down the humongous hill in Grandpa's backyard while Grandma cooked with Mom.

But when Dad left Mom to be in love with another woman, Mom told me that I was never allowed to speak to Dad's parents again, which I thought was unfair because they were my grandparents and we have a separate relationship.

I also used to love Thanksgiving because of the food. Grandma would make a huge turkey with gravy and stuffing, and everyone would make a big deal about Grandpa carving the turkey like he had a special skill that the rest of us could never learn.

But our neighbors, the Vegans, don't eat turkey or real gravy and they don't put marshmallows on top of their sweet potatoes because they said that marshmallows come from horse feet, which I didn't know and hope is a lie.

Not only do they not eat turkey, but the Vegans placed framed pictures of two turkeys on their Thanksgiving table with the turkeys' names underneath, which were "Mable" and "Todd." It was strange to see pictures of turkeys because no one ever really takes pictures of turkeys, and it was even stranger to see that they had names because no one really names turkeys, especially with a name like "Todd," which sounds like the name of a boy who asks the teacher for more homework.

All of the foods were labeled with little turkey-shaped signs, and I remembered the names carefully so that I know to avoid them in future Thanksgivings. The main foods were "Lentil and Mushroom Loaf with Savory Potato Filling" and "Stuffed Maple Tofu" and the side foods were "Gluten-Free(!) Spinach Roasted Fingerlings" and "King Oyster Whipped Sweet Potatoes with Herbs" (and without marshmallows).

Reading the weird names of the foods, I suddenly missed Dad and I thought that maybe Mom did too even though she always says that she hates him. I think that, even if you hate someone, it's easy to miss them on the holidays.

Before we were allowed to eat, we had to go around the room and say what we were thankful for. At Grandma and Grandpa's house we would do the same thing but more as a joke. It would always be funny and sarcastic, like Grandpa would say, "I'm thankful Grandma didn't burn the turkey like last year," and Grandma would say to Grandpa, "I'm thankful that you lost your teeth so that you'll only be able to eat the sweet potatoes."

But the Vegans said things that were sincere, like "family" and "togetherness," and Mom rolled her eyes at me and I rolled mine back at her and it made me feel good. I like it when Mom rolls her eyes with me because it's like having a silent secret with someone.

The Vegan Mom said she was thankful for her "enlightened consciousness" and that it was important to "keep turkeys, like Todd and Mable, in our hearts on this dark holiday." She said that turkeys are "beautiful and brilliant creatures who like music and dancing," which seemed kind of strange and probably not true. But then she described how the turkeys are killed and it made me feel really guilty and also nauseous. Before the turkeys are killed, she said, they are packed into tiny cages where they can't even turn around and, in order to make sure that the turkeys don't attack each other, they get their beaks and toes cut off with hot blades and then are boiled alive to get their feathers off. I pictured myself in a tight cage, not being able to turn around, and then getting my toes cut off and being boiled alive. Picturing yourself in someone else's life is called "empathy," which Mom says I have too much of.

I thought it was strange that the Vegan Mom described how turkeys were killed to a group of people who were about to eat tofu. It kind of felt like she was trying to sell me the shirt I was already wearing.

I don't totally think the Vegan people are so weird. In a way, it is more weird to eat a bird. We would all think it was disgusting to go outside and kill a bird and tear its head off and then stuff its body with croutons and celery and put it in an oven, but for some reason, we think it's normal to go to a supermarket and buy a turkey and cook it. I guess I'm being hypocritical by eating turkeys and I don't really know what to think about this.

I think it's really sad the way that animals are killed. But it's also really sad that I used to have Thanksgiving with my grandparents and now I'm not allowed to talk to them because Dad loves someone else. I guess that there are a lot of sad things in the world and sometimes eating turkey with the people you love makes you happy and maybe it would make the turkey happy to know that this was happening with its body. Probably not, but maybe.

If the turkey really liked music and dancing, maybe it would also like to know that I was rolling down Grandpa's hill with Dad and then eating its body. Probably not, but maybe. Maybe some things are too difficult for me to understand right now. Probably not, but maybe. That's why I'm giving the Vegan Thanksgiving 1000 out of 2000 stars.

MATTHEW'S HOUSE

Last night, I had dinner at Matthew's House, which Mom says is a "broken home" because Matthew's parents are divorced. When I asked Mom if we also lived in a broken home because she is divorced from Dad, she said, "No." When I asked her what the difference was, she said, "We still have money and all that woman has is rage and infertility."

I don't think Mom likes Matthew's mom. She always calls her "a slut with a bad nose job," but I just call her Paula because once I called her "Miss Fisher" and she said, "Just call me Paula."

I also think Mom doesn't like Matthew. She always makes weird jokes like, "In a few years, you two will finally be able to make honest men out of each other." I thought this was a weird thing to say because Matthew and I are almost always honest and Mom's the one who always lies. In fact, any time we're about to meet one of her friends, Mom gives me a list of lies I'm supposed to remember like, "Carol thinks I have a brother in the hospital in Cleveland," or "Denise doesn't know about the divorce, she thinks Dad is dead, just go with it."

Mom was right about Matthew and Paula not having any money. They don't even live in a real house; they live in a small weird building that's connected to other small weird buildings. Matthew calls it a "town house" but Mom calls it "the ghetto." When I asked Mom what a ghetto is, she told me to ask Esmeralda, the woman who cleans our house on Thursdays.

And they don't even own a car. Mom says that Paula gets "sympathy rides" to work in exchange for "HJs." When I asked Mom what an HJ was, she told me to ask Esmeralda.

Before dinner, Paula said, "Make sure you boys wash your paws," and Matthew growled like a lion and they both laughed. I wanted to ask them what they were talking about but I felt embarrassed.

Paula made a really nice dinner even though it's what Mom calls an "in-between" meal. An "in-between" meal is food that is not very fancy but also not very cheap. Mom says we shouldn't eat "in-between" meals. When I'm eating with Mom, we either eat a fancy meal, like when we go to a nice restaurant, or we eat a really cheap meal, like when Mom gives me a can of beans from the pantry and a peppermint candy from her purse for dessert. Mom says that the cheap meals allow us to eat the fancy ones more often and "in-between" meals are a waste.

But Paula's meal was "in-between" and also really good. For a salad, she made a basic salad with lettuce but she mixed in interesting fruits like slices of mandarin oranges and cranberries. It was actually really good and Paula said that one bowl of this salad will give us all the fruits and vegetables we need for the day. This seemed like a great idea but also made me think that I do not normally eat enough fruits or vegetables, and I didn't even realize that this was a thing I should be doing.

And for the main dinner, Paula made a quiche, which is like a serious version of pie. It had spinach and egg and cheese and it tasted so good that I asked for seconds, which is something Mom told me to not get in a habit of doing. The bottom of the quiche was doughy and so delicious and melted in my mouth and the sides were crusty like a cookie and the cheese and spinach were melty together in the fluffy egg. I know it sounds really weird but I actually liked the quiche more than real pie, which is what you're supposed like more.

When I told Paula how much I liked the quiche, she said in a weird voice that was supposed to sound like a pirate, "Aye, bucko. Ye sure know how to flatter a wench!"

I didn't know what she was talking about, so I just said, "Don't worry. I don't think you're a wench."

And then Matthew and Paula looked at each other strangely and laughed (at me, I think).

A few minutes later, when Matthew spilled a little soda on the table, Paula said again in her pirate voice, "Aye! Now you're going to the brig, matey!"

And then Matthew said, also in a pirate voice, "Argh! Just when me hunger is arousing the most!"

And then Paula said, in a different pirate voice, "Ye best be getting a napkin from ye sink to clean up this here soda!"

Then Matthew said something else in a pirate voice and then they were both talking in pirate voices and laughing.

I thought that I should maybe talk like a pirate too, but I never practiced that voice so I thought it might come out wrong. And I couldn't tell if they were laughing at the pirate voice or the lines they were saying, and I was worried that if I just did the voice but didn't say the right pirate lines, they would think I was stupid.

And the weirdest part was that Matthew was my best friend but I never heard him do a pirate voice before. Sometimes at school, he pretends he's a rich woman from the South and it's so funny. He waves his hand in front of his face like it's an old-timey fan and says, "That gentleman caller saw me before I put my face on, bless his heart! Now I have the vapors!" It's so funny.

But every time Matthew did the pirate voice to Paula, I felt like a "third wheel," which is an expression I recently learned from Mom. After Dad left Mom, Mom didn't want to go out to dinner with any of her married friends because she said it made her feel like a "third wheel." When I asked her what this meant, she told me that a third wheel is "someone who no one loves." And I could tell that Mom felt really bad about being the third wheel so, the next morning, while Mom was still asleep, I took my tricycle out of the garage and brought it up to her bedroom. And I made a little sign that said, YOU'RE A THIRD WHEEL BUT I LOVE YOU, and I put it on the seat of the tricycle. And when Mom woke up, she called me into the bedroom and she was crying and she hugged me and told me that I was "very sweet" but that I should "take the bike out of the room immediately because it was tracking dirt."

This is something Mom always does. She says something nice to me and then yells at me right after. Like she couldn't just say, "You're very sweet." She had to say, "You're very sweet but take the bike out of my room." And even though it should make my feelings hurt to be yelled at, I also like it because it's a pattern that Mom and I have, and it's ours. And I think it's kind of similar to the pirate voices. Every relationship has a kind of pattern, I guess, and maybe the pattern is more important than the stuff that makes up the pattern. Like the pirate voice is more important than the pirate lines.

And I guess even if someone is a terrible person like Mom, they can still be special if you know them well. Like Paula is really normal and doesn't yell or curse at me, but she's not My Mother. And sometimes knowing someone really well is more important than liking them. That's why I'm giving Matthew's House 219 out of 2000 stars.

FUDDRUCKERS AND AN UNRELIABLE NEW FRIEND

Yesterday, Matthew and I went to Fuddruckers, which is a place that sounds like a swear word but actually just sells disgusting hamburgers that you have to make yourself.

We were supposed to meet someone named Lyle that Matthew met on the Internet. Lyle told Matthew to meet him at Fuddruckers at three o'clock but Matthew insisted that we get there a few minutes early, "just to be polite." And Lyle told us to come alone, not with our parents, which was fine for me because Mom has been encouraging me to have experiences that "don't include" her. But Matthew had to lie to his mother so he told her that we had to stay after school for a science project.

As soon as school ended Matthew grabbed my arm and we snuck out the back door, past the buses, and started walking to Fuddruckers. On the way, Matthew wouldn't stop talking about his new friend Lyle. They met on the Internet because they were both fans of the band Serial 17, which isn't even a real band. Serial 17 is just four teenage boys who sing but play no instruments, and Mom taught me that bands like that shouldn't be called bands because "they only exist to boost the heart rates of fat girls and pederasts."

Anyway, Lyle is the president of the Serial 17 fan club and he started emailing Matthew after Matthew posted a picture of himself at a concert. Matthew kept saying that Lyle was "so funny" and "so mature" and that he knew all the lyrics to every Serial 17 song. I wanted to say, "That's easy. All their songs sound exactly the same," but I didn't want to hurt Matthew's feelings so I just said, "Cool."

Matthew had never actually met Lyle in person and I was happy he was taking me to their first meeting, but also a little annoyed by how much Matthew seemed to like him. I know it probably sounds weird to say this, but the more Matthew talked about Lyle the more I started to hate Lyle.

I knew why Matthew liked him so much. It's easy to like someone on the Internet. When you're with someone in person you have to see all of their weird things. Like Matthew cracks his knuckles and it's kind of annoying. If Lyle knew that Matthew cracked his knuckles maybe he wouldn't like him, but I know about it and still like him, so that means our friendship is real.

We got to Fuddruckers at exactly three o'clock and I could tell that Matthew was a little annoyed with me for walking slowly because he said, "You seem like you're kind of out of shape." We looked around but there was no other boy sitting alone, so Matthew and I got a table by the window and waited for Lyle. I could tell that Matthew was nervous so I asked, "Do you want me to build us burgers?" because at Fuddruckers you have to build your own burger. But Matthew kind of scowled at me and said in a mean voice, "How would that look to Lyle?"

I was thinking about how that would look to Lyle when we heard police sirens. I looked outside and saw four police cars screech into the parking lot. Matthew ducked under the table and said, "My mom found out I'm not at school!"

But then I saw why the police were there: they were forcing a man onto the ground, facedown, and putting him in handcuffs. It was so strange to see somebody be arrested in real life. Usually on TV the person getting arrested is struggling and yelling at the police, but this man was just calmly lying on the ground. Almost like he was *waiting* to be arrested.

Matthew started cracking his knuckles. And, for some reason, it calmed me down.

But then the weirdest thing of all happened. The man stood up in the handcuffs, turned to me and Matthew, saw us through the window, and *smiled* right at us. It gave us the willies at the same time. The man was so creepy! He was wearing baggy sweatpants and a sweatshirt and there were wet stains on them, like he'd been wearing them for a long time or eating TV dinners in them.

I whispered to Matthew, "Let's never come here again." And Matthew whispered back, "I can't wait to tell Lyle about this!"

After the man got taken away, Matthew and I got burgers

and waited for Lyle, who never showed up. I was actually relieved, but I didn't want to make Matthew feel bad so I said,
"He probably just got busy with Serial 17 stuff."

And Matthew said, "Yeah, he's the president. Did I tell you
that?"

And I wanted to say, "Yes! You told me that a million
times!" But instead, I just said, "Cool."

Matthew looked at his watch and said, "If he's not here in
the next fifteen minutes we can go." So Matthew and I waited
but I had a feeling Lyle was not going to show up.

And it was actually kind of nice to just sit with Matthew.
I realized that we hadn't done that in a while and it made me
think that it didn't matter if Matthew liked Lyle. Even if you're
best friends with someone on the Internet, you can't just sit
with them quietly. And sometimes, when Matthew and I are
just sitting with each other quietly, I like him the most. Matthew will crack his knuckles, and even though it makes me
nauseous, it also makes me feel like I'm real.

That's why I'm giving Fuddruckers 1062 out of 2000 stars
and Lyle 97 out of 2000 stars.

A CRAWFISH BOIL AND
DAD'S NEW FAMILY

Last week I visited Dad and his new family in New Orleans, Louisiana, which is a town that Dad says proves that "poor people are happier than rich people." And every day I was there, we had the exact same thing for lunch: a crawfish boil.

A crawfish boil is where you put a lot of weird creatures that look like a cross between shrimps and spiders into a huge pot of boiling water with garlic and corn and potatoes. Then you take the dead crawfish out, remove their heads, peel back their tails, and eat the middle part of their bodies. It takes a really long time to eat a tiny bit of chewy meat.

And I think the crawfish boil is kind of like Dad's new life in New Orleans: he works really hard for a tiny reward.

This is what happened to Dad:

When Dad left me and Mom, he moved to New Orleans to

"find himself." I didn't know what that meant, but Mom said he was really just trying to find some "hotter, dumber woman who would steal his money in exchange for making him think he's still attractive."

But Dad's new girlfriend, Izzy, is not dumb and she is definitely not prettier than Mom: she has short hair like a man and weird teeth and wears men's clothes, like dirty boots and ripped jeans. And she runs a big company that builds houses for poor people who lost their homes in a hurricane. When Dad moved to New Orleans, he started building houses for Izzy's company as a volunteer and then fell in love with Izzy, which seems hard because of her hair, teeth, and clothes, but I guess she was easier to love than Mom, who was always yelling at him. Now, Izzy and Dad run the company together and take care of Izzy's son, Edgar, who is five years old and not a good person.

And Izzy definitely didn't like Dad for his money because they lived like homeless people if homeless people were allowed to have homes and still be called homeless. Their house was really ugly and small and rotting and their backyard was overgrown with weeds and broken potted plants. I thought it was interesting that they lived like this because their job is rebuilding other people's houses. It almost seemed like they were punishing themselves for not losing their house in a hurricane.

And it was weird to see Dad in his new life. He looked older *and* younger than I remember. He had a beard and his face was tan and wrinkly, but he also seemed calm and his body seemed like it had more energy in it. And I think I never saw him smile before but it was actually kind of creepy because it was a familiar face doing an unfamiliar thing. And when he hugged me I felt a little weird because it felt like a stranger was hugging me. He squeezed me really hard and held me for a long time, but not in a way that felt like he meant it, but in a way that felt like he was trying to make up for the last year when he didn't visit or hug me once. I tried to pat his back because I thought it might end the hug but he just started patting my back. Then we were both just squeezing each other and patting each other's backs, but I was doing it to end the hug and Dad was doing it to keep the hug going.

Dad said that Izzy was out building a poor person's house and that she would be back in time for lunch, which was going to be a crawfish boil (surprise, surprise!) in the backyard. Then Izzy's son, Edgar, came running through the house like a dog that just got let out of a cage. He was five years old but he acted much younger and was very dirty and didn't make eye contact and always had some dried snot hanging out of his nose that he sometimes licked by sticking his tongue high out of his mouth and trying to reach the snot. Seeing this made me nauseous.

I thought I might feel jealous of Edgar because Dad was now taking care of him and not me, but when I saw Dad with Edgar I just felt sad for Edgar. Dad seemed to pretend Edgar didn't even exist. He just let him run around the house knocking into things and he didn't even introduce him to me. And I started to remember that Dad used to act the same way to me but I never noticed it because he was my dad and I was used to it. I guess sometimes it's easier to see how people act when it's not happening to you.

When Izzy came home, Dad tried to give her a hug but she said, "I'm filthy," and walked straight into the bathroom. When we heard the water turn on, Dad turned to me, smiling in an embarrassed kind of way, and said, "That's Izzy."

All three crawfish lunches were the exact same experience: Izzy and Dad talked about the poor people whose houses they were rebuilding and how sad the hurricane was while Edgar ran around us, holding the dead crawfishes like they were monsters trying to attack us. Dad and Izzy just ignored Edgar, which was probably the reason he had no social skills, but they also ignored me, which just made me feel left out.

Dad never asked me anything about myself or school and he definitely didn't ask about Mom. The only thing he would say to me was "Can you believe that?" after he would say something sad about the hurricane, like how many people drowned or why the government didn't like the black people because of racism.

And I thought it was strange because a part of me wanted to be angry at Dad for not asking me about myself, but I also felt guilty being angry at him because he was ignoring me to talk about something sad. And I guess I felt like he was doing a good thing by rebuilding the houses, but I thought it was weird how he felt so much for the strangers in New Orleans but nothing for me who is his son.

And then I started thinking about Mom, who is kind of the opposite of Dad. She spends every day doing selfish things and doesn't help anybody who's poor, and when we pass a homeless person on the street, she holds her nose like she might get sick if she smells them. And she's not even that nice to me, but at least she treats me like I exist.

I guess if I was a homeless person from New Orleans, I would like Dad more than Mom. But I'm just a kid from the suburbs and that's not my fault.

And that's why I'm giving the crawfish boil and Dad and Izzy and Edgar 213 out of 2000 stars.

MUSEUM OF NATURAL HISTORY

Yesterday we took a class trip to the Museum of Natural History, which is a place where you're supposed to learn about history but all you really do is look at dinosaur skeletons and eat lunch. And it's so strange because it's really sad to see the dinosaur skeletons because not only are *those* dinosaurs dead but *all* dinosaurs are dead. It was kind of like visiting a cemetery, but instead of everyone being buried, their bones were above the ground and held together like they were still trying to be alive.

But instead of feeling sad for the dinosaurs or just being quiet like you're supposed to do at a funeral, all the kids were making jokes and acting stupid. And even though the dinosaurs were scary and would probably eat me if they were alive, I started to feel bad for them.

The woman who works for the museum explained that there were three different kinds of dinosaurs: some were carnivores, which means they ate the other dinosaurs, some were herbivores, which means they were nice and didn't eat each other, and some were omnivores, which means they ate everything. Billy, a kid in my class, is an omnivore because he will literally eat anything on a dare. Last week, he ate an entire pack of gum, even the wrapper, and then threw up and got to miss gym.

The dinosaurs were also very mean to each other. They would fight and use their mouths and teeth and claws to attack each other. The Tyrannosaurus Rex was the meanest one. He looked the meanest and his name sounded the meanest and he ate all the other dinosaurs. The one who was the nicest was the Apatosaurus because he was really big but he had a tiny little head and he never ate any other dinosaurs. And I thought it must have been scary to be an Apatosaurus because he just wanted to be nice but there was probably a lot of pressure to be mean because he was a dinosaur.

All the kids wanted to take pictures in front of the dinosaur skeletons and they were laughing and making stupid faces like they were imitating the dinosaurs. I started to imagine the dinosaurs coming alive and watching the kids do this in front of their dead bones and I suddenly got angry for them. I asked the museum lady if I could go to the bathroom and she said it was okay and that I should meet everyone back in the Museum Cafeteria. Usually we're supposed to bring a buddy to the bathroom but I didn't really feel like I had a buddy, so I went alone and waited in the stall until lunchtime.

In the Museum Cafeteria, everyone got dinosaur-shaped chicken nuggets, which were like regular chicken nuggets but formed into the bodies of dinosaurs. I thought it was strange to eat dinosaur-shaped chicken because the dinosaurs were dead and it felt like we were making fun of them by eating their bodies in fun-looking shapes. So I just got a peanut butter and jelly sandwich and then Billy called me a faggot, which means gay. I wanted to tell him that he's a faggot too because he was eating the body of a dinosaur, but I didn't want to say the word "faggot" because it sounds mean so I just looked down at my sandwich and sort of lost my appetite. I think if Billy was a dinosaur he would be a Tyrannosaurus Rex and I would be an Apatosaurus and I wouldn't try to hurt him but I would also not be bullied because the Apatosaurus is much bigger than the Tyrannosaurus Rex.

On the bus ride home, everyone was texting each other the pictures of themselves doing funny things in front of the dinosaurs. Mark Schwartz made it look like he was picking a Stegosaurus's nose by standing close to the camera and sticking his finger up. Madison Greenwood was pretending to dance with a Triceratops' leg. Even Matthew took a picture doing a split with his arms stretched out like a bird underneath a Pterodactyl. I thought it was weird because Matthew usually behaves better. Sometimes he does bad things to fit in, but I think this is probably because he doesn't fully know which dinosaur he wants to be yet.

Everyone was laughing at the pictures together and I started to feel a little lonely, like I wasn't involved with the group or like everyone was laughing at a joke that I couldn't hear. And I thought that maybe I should have eaten the dinosaur-shaped chicken nuggets and taken a picture in front of a dinosaur doing something stupid. I would have been uncomfortable for a few minutes but it would mean that I would have been able to fit in with my friends. Or maybe I would have had a bathroom buddy. Or maybe I wouldn't have had to hide in the bathroom at all.

And I guess it's like what the dinosaurs had to do. They probably didn't want to always be so angry and they probably definitely didn't want to eat each other, but I guess, if you want to be part of a group, you have to make compromises sometimes. And I guess, in that way, we aren't that much different from the dinosaurs. And even though we think we're better and smarter because we wear clothes and speak English, maybe we're all just trying to fit in even though it means we sometimes have to do things that make us uncomfortable. That's why I'm giving the Museum of Natural History 1109 out of 2000 stars.

THE ASHRAM AND MOM

Over the weekend, Mom took me to an Ashram, which is a place that stressed-out people go when they're rich. We were supposed to stay for the whole weekend but we ended up sneaking out in the middle of the first night, which sounds like a bad thing to do but it was also the most fun thing that Mom and I ever did together.

When we first arrived at the Ashram, I knew we probably wouldn't last the whole weekend. There was a sign at the front entrance that said, REPEAL YOUR VANITY, RELEASE YOUR POSSESSIONS, RELEARN TO LIVE. I knew Mom would not want to do any of these three things. We had just spent the whole week shopping for sexy yoga outfits for Mom to wear at the Ashram and she was definitely not planning on repealing or releasing any of these.

I don't even know why Mom wanted to go to the Ashram. She kept saying that she just needed some "Me Time," which seems like a strange thing to need, but even more strange because Mom spends every day taking "Me Time" because she has no job and drinks alcohol every night to go to sleep.

But Mom put on a fake smile, which has become her only kind of smile, grabbed our suitcase, and said, "Wake me up when it's over."

The Ashram was made up of several buildings that were kind of like old-timey cabins surrounding a big pool. At the front was a check-in building and, when Mom and I entered, there was a woman behind the counter who had dreadlocks for hair even though she was a white woman. I could see Mom hide a face of hatred for this woman, especially when the woman said, "*Namaste* and welcome to the first step toward inner harmony. Our spiritual founder, Satchidananda, once observed, 'Truth is one, Paths are many.' Nonetheless, we were rated as the best ashram in the Northern Lakes region by *Wellness Magazine* two years in a row. Welcome, *Namaste.*"

I could sense right there that Mom wanted to escape from what she quickly realized was a kind of prison, but she smiled a fake smile again and said, "*Namaste*, thank you, we're checking in."

The white woman with dreadlocks proceeded to tell us about the Ashram and the rules we had to follow, which all sounded like things that Mom hates. We had to wake up every morning at 5:45 for a *satsang*, which is a meeting with the other guests of the Ashram. Mom asked if she could just send me to the meeting to take notes and report back, but the woman said that it was mandatory, which is one of the words that Mom hates.

The woman also said that we were not allowed to use our cell phones and that we had to put all of our "material possessions" into a "Trust Locker," which were little cubbyholes. Mom said a "Trust Locker" is something that is called an oxymoron, like "Happily Married." Then she laughed in a kind of fake way and the woman and I just stared at each other waiting for her to stop.

Mom then asked the woman, "What happens if someone steals our stuff from the Trust Locker?" And the woman said, "Then you'll be one possession freer." Mom nodded and said, "I think I'll just hold on to it for now." And the dreadlocked white woman said, "I'm sorry to hear you're still bound."

Our room was near the back of the Ashram and next to the large pool. The pool, the woman explained, was "clothing optional." And apparently, everyone in the pool chose the "naked" option, and Mom and I could see their privates as they sat around the pool, casually talking to each other like they weren't naked.

It was actually disgusting to see all of the men and women with their weird penises and floppy breasts. I normally would have found it funny to see naked people in a pool outside my room, but for some reason I just felt really strange looking at them, like when you walk in on someone going to the bathroom.

Mom and I finally got to our room and closed the door. Mom stared at me in a really intense way like we just got out of a war together. I wanted to tell her that we should leave, that this place was scary and weird, and that she could have "Me Time" at home if she wanted to and that I would promise not to bother her all weekend or ask for anything if she would just take me home.

But Mom just put on a fake smile and said, "Yoga's in an hour. And then dinner." Then she walked into the bathroom and shut the door.

Yoga was held outside, next to the Penis Pool. Everyone gathered in a really serious way onto Indian-looking mats that were spread out. The mats were damp from sweat and smelled like a wet dog, and we had to take our shoes off, which made me feel gross.

Mom wore really tight gray spandex pants and a little pink shirt that didn't cover her belly all the way. And I think she thought she looked sexy in her short shirt, but her belly fat poked out from the bottom and made her look fatter than she actually is, which is not really that fat.

A man with a long beard who looked homeless was the yoga teacher and he was wearing orange pants and necklaces instead of a shirt. He started by giving a speech about how we have all gathered here today to focus inwardly and re-learn to move like a baby, which kind of made me laugh because I pictured everyone there crawling around the sweaty mats like babies. Then he told us that we had to think about the real things in our lives and forget about our material possessions. He told us to focus on the important relationships in our lives and how we are all connected to energy and other people.

Then he made us all bend down and do weird positions and everyone seemed to know what they were doing, even Mom. And while everyone was bending down with their eyes closed, I stood up and looked around and suddenly realized that I was the only kid in the whole group.

Then it occurred to me that maybe Mom didn't actually want me to come here; none of the other people brought their children. Maybe Mom only brought me because, as part of their divorce, Dad agreed to pay for any activity Mom did with me. Maybe that's why she took me to nice restaurants and on vacations and to the Ashram. I tried to put this thought out of my mind because it didn't do anything good, but it wouldn't really leave. The homeless yoga teacher wanted us to focus on our relationships, but my main relationship was Mom and I started to worry that maybe it wasn't even real.

After yoga, we had to gather in the biggest cabin for dinner. Everyone was still sweating and smelled like sweat and had sweat on their feet, but I was happy to be done with the yoga and I was really hungry.

All through dinner, though, I still had the weird feeling in my head that maybe Mom only took me around so Dad would pay for her. I kept telling this thought to go away, but for some reason bad thoughts always stay longer than good thoughts.

And the food was so disgusting. It was all vegetarian, which I usually don't mind, but it was the bad kind of vegetarian food, where they put so much spice on everything to try to make you forget that it's not meat.

The fork was made of a carrot cut into the shape of a fork and we had to eat the fork after eating the meal so that there was no waste. And the bowl was made from seaweed, which tastes like when you accidentally swallow dirty ocean water. Seaweed is something fish might like to eat because they have limited options underwater, but humans have other things that are better like waffles and grapes. But I was so distracted by my bad thoughts that I couldn't really focus on how gross the food was.

Mom and I walked back to our room after dinner but we didn't really talk that much. I think we were both a little homesick and I didn't want to ask Mom about my fear. I guess I was scared that it might be true and, even if she lied to me and told me that she took me everywhere with her because she loved me, I would probably know that she was lying. Mom lies all the time and it's usually easy to tell because she overdoes it.

When we got back to the room, Mom said, "Great day, huh?" which was a lie. I almost wanted to cry because I wanted her to at least say, "Yoga was weird. The Indian carpet was sweaty. The Penis Pool is disgusting. And the food was gross." I wanted her to say at least one true thing but for some reason she needed to lie. And I wanted to say, "No! It was a terrible day. I hate it here." But for some reason, I felt I had to lie as well. I don't know why. I think I felt that if I said anything true, I would immediately start crying. So I just said, "Yeah, I love it here."

And then we didn't say anything else to each other all night and we just went to sleep, which was hard for me because I couldn't get the bad thoughts out of my head. Nighttime can be really scary if you're worried about something.

During the day, there are all sorts of things to distract you, like people and daylight, but if you're worried about something at nighttime, it seems like it's the only thing in the whole world.

And I kept worrying that maybe my whole life was fake. Like if Mom was my main relationship and it was fake, then what did I have that was real? I'm friends with Matthew, but sometimes that feels fake too. And I liked Dad but he turned fake and moved away. Sometimes I worry that the only thing I really have is myself and that's a really scary thought.

I must have finally fallen asleep because the next thing I remember was really weird: a loud bell started ringing and I opened my eyes to see Mom standing above my bed, wide-awake. Her hair was wet from excited sweating and she looked wild-eyed. She said, "It's 5:45. We can either go to the morning meeting and spend the whole day doing yoga and eating carrot forks or we can get the hell out of here. Your call."

I didn't even have to say anything. I just nodded, so relieved! And Mom smiled, so relieved as well. Then we grabbed all of our stuff and crammed it into our suitcase and darted out of the room.

We ran around the Penis Pool, over the sweaty carpets, past the Trust Lockers, and finally into the parking lot. We jumped into the car and, as Mom started the engine, the dreadlocked white woman ran out of the welcome building and called after us, "You're going to miss *satsang!*"

And Mom rolled down her window and shouted back, "Trust me, I'm not!"

And then the woman said, "We're sorry to see you're not

spiritually aligned enough to make it through the whole weekend."

And then Mom said, "Fuck off!" and pulled out of the parking lot.

And even though Mom cursed, I started laughing, which is not normal for me because usually when Mom curses it makes me feel like I have a Sister instead of a Mother. But for some reason, I couldn't stop laughing. Maybe because it was so early or maybe because I was just so happy to leave the Ashram, but I laughed until my cheeks hurt.

As we were driving home, the sun began to rise and I stared at Mom, who seemed kind of happy for the first time since Dad left. She opened the window and let the air blow her wet hair back, which is something she never does because she doesn't like fresh air.

And I started laughing again because I suddenly thought that, a long time ago, Mom was a child like me. I never realized that Mom had her own life before me and maybe she was happy as a child or maybe she was sad, but she probably didn't think that one day she would be so angry.

Mom asked me, "What are you laughing at?"

And I said the truth: "I thought of you as a child."

And then Mom started smiling. And I almost didn't recognize her smile because it was a real smile. And it made her face look different—her eyes squinted and her cheeks puffed out a little. And even though she looked older than when she fake smiles, she looked a lot better.

And then she said, "I was actually a really pretty girl."

And she had tears in her eyes even though she was smiling.

And then I had tears in my eyes even though I was smiling too.

And I wanted to ask her if she only took me around so that Dad would pay for her but I already knew the answer: Mom took me around because she needed me.

Because going through a hard life with someone else is better than going through an easy life alone.

That's why I'm giving the Ashram 27 out of 2000 stars and Mom 1892 out of 2000 stars.

II.
FAMILY

MY LITTLE SISTER TEXTS ME
WITH HER PROBLEMS

MY SISTER: Hey u up?

ME: It's four in the morning.

MY SISTER: Yeah.

ME: Are you okay?

MY SISTER: No!

ME: Why?

MY SISTER: Micah's being a total dick.

ME: Did he hurt you?

MY SISTER: What? No. He's just being a dick.

ME: Oh. So can we talk about this in the morning?

MY SISTER: CAN YOU STOP ATTACKING ME?

ME: I'm not attacking you. So what happened?

MY SISTER: We were supposed to just stay in tonight because

Wednesday is our quiet night and he invited Jarred over, who's a pothead but like the selfish kind and the two of them were just making dumb jokes the whole night and I felt totally invisible.

ME: Do you want me to talk to him?

MY SISTER: Who?

ME: Micah.

MY SISTER: What? No! Why?

ME: To tell him to be nicer or something?

MY SISTER: WHAT??

ME: I don't know. Is he there with you?

MY SISTER: Yeah. He's sleeping. So sweet!

ME: So it's okay between you two?

MY SISTER: YES! STOP IT!

ME: Okay. I'm gonna go back to sleep now.

MY SISTER: FINE!

ME: Night honey.

MY SISTER: I love you! Call me sometime! I miss you!

MY SISTER: Hey u up?

ME: I am now.

MY SISTER: Have you bought mom a birthday thing yet?

ME: A birthday thing?

MY SISTER: Like a present?

ME: Oh. Yeah. I did.

MY SISTER: WHAT? WHY!?

ME: Cause it's her birthday. Can we talk about this in the morning?

MY SISTER: NO! Dad's being a total dick. He's like "your mother's not turning 60 again. Do you think she wants to remember this as the birthday you didn't get her a present?"

ME: Well why didn't you get her anything?

MY SISTER: BECAUSE I'VE BEEN BUSY?! CAN YOU PLEASE NOT ATTACK ME RIGHT NOW?

ME: I wasn't attacking you.

MY SISTER: What did you get her?

ME: I got her a small giraffe statue. Like the one she liked from that antique place in New Hope.

MY SISTER: Can you say it's from both of us?

ME: Okay, do you want to split it?

MY SISTER: Well how much $ was it?

ME: Like 200?

[NO RESPONSE]

ME: Okay, I'll say it's from both.

MY SISTER: Thx. And call me sometime! I feel like we never talk!

MY SISTER: Hey u up?

ME: No.

MY SISTER: Having major crisis!

ME: K. What?

MY SISTER: 25 pg paper due in four hrs!!! Professor's being a total dick.

ME: Do you need any help?

MY SISTER: Do you know anything about Cameroonian separatists?

ME: No.

MY SISTER: Then no.

ME: So can I go back to sleep?

MY SISTER: NO! I'm distraught!

ME: Why?

MY SISTER: They want to start their own govt in the south which is totally fine but the Cameroonian Loyalists don't want them to because it would include the oil-rich Bakassi peninsula! So UNFAIR!

ME: Uh huh.

MY SISTER: And the Loyalists already ADMITTED that it didn't belong to them! It's like, JUST LEAVE THE AM-BAZONIA REGION ALREADY!!!

ME: Right. I'm really tired.

MY SISTER: It's total domestic neocolonialism and it's like, HELLO! GIVE THEM THE POLITICAL SOVER-EIGNTY THEY DESERVE UNLESS YOU WANT AN-OTHER RWANDA ON YOUR HANDS!!!

ME: Sure. It's just I kind of have a big day tomorrow.

MY SISTER: Okay fine! Go to sleep.

ME: Thx. Good luck with the paper.

MY SISTER: Don't patronize me

ME: I wasn't patronizing you.

ME: Hello?

MY SISTER: Hey u up?

ME: Haven't heard from you in a few days.

MY SISTER: I know sry bout that.

ME: No it's been good actually. I finally got some sleep. Lol.

MY SISTER: Can you please not joke now?!

ME: Oh. Sorry.

MY SISTER: Not in the mood!

ME: Okay why?

MY SISTER: I was taken hostage by the Cameroonian Loyalists and just got cell service.

ME: What?!

MY SISTER: They read my paper.

ME: Are you serious?

MY SISTER: And Cameroonian Prime Minister Philemon Yunji Yang is being a total dick. Telling me that I can't leave till I take back what I wrote! It's like FREEDOM OF SPEECH, you know?

ME: Oh my god! Should I call the embassy?

MY SISTER: NO! They make such a big deal. And DON'T TELL MOM! She always overreacts. Remember when I was vegan?? Argh!

ME: Are you in danger?

MY SISTER: It's like, I'LL EAT WHATEVER I WANT, MOM!

ME: Okay. But Are You Safe???

MY SISTER: STOP ATTACKING ME! YES! I'm safe. I'm just pissed off.

ME: Okay. So can we talk about this when you get home?

MY SISTER: Yeah, can you pick me up from JFK when I'm released?

ME: Sure, send me your flight details.

MY SISTER: And don't just drive around the terminal. Actually park and come in and get me ;-)

ME: K.

MY SISTER: Thx. I love you. CALL ME SOMETIME!

SEPARATION ANXIETY SLEEPAWAY CAMP

8 A.M. Campers begin the day with an early call to Mom. Those campers who have wet the bed will have an opportunity to change clothes or, if they prefer, to remain in their soiled pajamas as the warm stench of their own urine may be more comforting and remind them of home.

9 A.M. Breakfast is served in the main dining hall, though most campers will choose not to eat breakfast, as it is hard to eat first thing in the morning because the day hasn't started and this thought is mortifying. Those campers who boldly choose to eat will be given pancakes in the shape of their names, which will remind them of home and likely cause indigestion.

10:30 A.M. Swim time. Campers will swim for seven minutes in a shallow wading pool, with two lifeguards per camper. Campers will wear pre-inflated floaties on their arms and legs and around their necks. After swim, campers will have an opportunity to call their mom to let her know that they have not drowned.

If the camper has drowned, Mothers will be notified by the Counselors in Training, or CITs. The Counselors in Training will then have an opportunity call their own Mothers.

NOON. Lunchtime. Campers dig into one of Mom's prepackaged lunches. Campers are encouraged not to read enclosed notes until after food is digested, which will be difficult as the thought of the unread note will be unsettling.

Following lunch, campers are given a free reading period, in which they may read their notes from Mom. If a camper has not received a note from Mom, one of the Counselors in Training, or "CITs," will forge a note and pretend it was lost in the refrigerator that housed the campers' lunches. Attempts to match Mom's handwriting will be sincerely made, although complete accuracy cannot be guaranteed.

2–3 P.M. Campers will be given a "free period" where they will have one hour to explore the campgrounds, kayak on nearby Lake Winooski, build a campfire, or write a postcard to their Mom. Calls to Mom are also possible during this time.

4 P.M. We follow free period with an afternoon call to Mom. At this point, campers may also ask to speak to their father, but

this is strictly optional. Most likely, Dad will not have time for the camper or, if he does have time, will likely talk about himself and how stressful work is or how well the camper's sister is doing in her sports camp. If Dad is spoken to during this period, campers will be allotted twenty additional minutes to debrief with Mom. Tissues provided.

5:30 P.M. Campers may choose from a variety of electives including Show-and-Tell, where campers can present a relic from their home to their fellow campers, who will likely not be able to focus on something from someone else's life as this requires a level of interest in others that campers do not possess during periods of great agitation.

Campers may also choose Arts and Crafts, where campers can draw family portraits wherein the Mother figure is unconsciously drawn much larger than the Father figure, who will likely have an X drawn, again unconsciously, through his face.

We will also be featuring a new elective this year, called "Lamentation Period," where campers are given time to reflect on their relationship with their mother and lament the futility of life away from home and the terror that accompanies leaving the house. Fears of college can also be prematurely contemplated during this time.

7 P.M. Dinner is served in the main dining hall. Campers are encouraged to eat freely as the day is almost over and they are one day closer to being home. Though it is optional, campers may even enjoy themselves briefly and, if desired, experience

the slightest amount of relief that they are a few hours closer to going home than they were at breakfast.

AT 9 P.M., it is lights out. Unless a camper would like to stay up all night and call their mom. If this is the case, a call to Mom is possible at this, or any, time. If the camper chooses to sleep but then has a nightmare, a call to Mom is allowed and encouraged. If the camper chooses to sleep but wakes up before his bunkmates, the camper may call his mother. If the camper chooses to sleep and makes it through the whole night without a call to Mom, he will be escorted home by one of the Counselors in Training, or "CITs," to apologize to his mom for being aloof.

Counselors in Training will be made up of campers' moms.

MY MOTHER EXPLAINS
THE BALLET TO ME

Where have you been? It's starting in five minutes! I hate having to leave your ticket at the box office. Why can't you just show up on time like a normal person? You think you'd be able to be here early since you're not coming from a job, a girlfriend, any kind of rich social life or commitment to public service. Anyway, I'm glad you're here. Give me a kiss.

What did you think of that usher? She seems pretty, a little chunky maybe, but nice, right? A nice face. You need to find someone like that. Did you like her? Did you say anything to her or did you just nod and shut down like you do around any girl that's not Sarah? Anyway, she is a bit chunky. Not for you.

O.K., it's starting. Do you know anything about this ballet? It was $125, you should know what you're seeing. It was written by Wagner, which is pronounced *"Vag-ner"* and who was a Nazi but before Hitler. O.K., turn your phone off. It's starting.

You see, what's happening now is that she's in love with those three men. That's why they're all holding roses. And she's courting them at the same time. Like when you drove all the way to Providence for Sarah's graduation and she decided she didn't have any time for you. But I'm sure she was able to squeeze in some time for what's-his-name. Patrick? Are they still together? They deserve each other. She was never right for you. She brought almond cake to the house after your grandmother's funeral. As if one death in the family wasn't enough, she wants me to go into anaphylactic shock at my own mother-in-law's funeral? I'm not telling you who you should date, it's not my business and I respect your "process," but that girl was an ungrateful hussy who never appreciated you.

Why can't you stand like that guy on stage? Look at his posture. Forget that he's black for a second and just look at his body. His shoulders are back. He has confidence. You look like you're apologizing even before you open your mouth. You walk in a room, no one notices. He walks on stage, we're all looking. Look at him, he's like a walking picture. I never dated a black man. Your father was so attractive in college. It stifled me, in a way. I used to be very progressive.

Stop nodding off. What did you do all day that you're so tired? Are you sweating? You smell like you're sweating.

Look who she's dancing with now. *Quelle surprise!* You see? When you stand up straight, she takes your rose. It's just about the confidence you project. If you had confidence, people would notice you. There was a kid in a wheelchair back in Elmhurst but he was so funny, he knew how to laugh at himself and, in a way, we all liked him.

What she's doing now is called a *pas de chat*. It's French and we all know how you did in that class, so I'll just solve the mystery and tell you that it means "step of the cat."

Ah, look at that! She just fell! Ha! Clumsy. I could do that. "Step of the cat." I used to dance, did I tell you that? I could've been successful if I hadn't had your sister. She tore my body apart. She's still destroying me, in a way. I could've done that. It looks harder than it is.

Oh, he's back! Look at him! He's an Adonis. Do you think he puts something in his pants to fill it out? No one has such a big thing, right? Your father is the only man I've ever been with. Can you believe that? It's noble, in a way, but I'm not going to Heaven for not having any fun.

Can you please pay attention for a second? Your fidgeting is distracting me. I understand you're impatient. I've been impatient too. Like when I was impatient for thirty-six hours while you took your sweet time ambling down my birth canal. That wasn't exactly fun for me either. It felt like I was trying to shit out a watermelon. Had I known about the size of your head, I would've gotten a Caesarean. Hindsight, right?

Okay, what's happening now is we're being kicked out because I'm talking too much. The usher, who I initially thought was pretty—Hi, dear!—is escorting us out. And understandably so, I haven't stopped audibly insulting you since this started and it's distracting to the other patrons. She is actually cute up close. A little flabby in the neck, but cute. Try to get her number.

Listen, I can't drive you home, you'll have to take the train. Traffic is a nightmare at the tunnel right now.

I'll see you next week. Try to be on time. I think it was a great idea that we got these season tickets. Give me a kiss. Love you, sweetheart.

AN EMAIL EXCHANGE WITH MY FIRST GIRLFRIEND, WHICH AT A CERTAIN POINT IS TAKEN OVER BY MY OLDER SISTER, A COLLEGE STUDENT STUDYING THE BOSNIAN GENOCIDE

ME: hey amy . . . just got home from food shopping with my mother. She takes FOREVER in every aisle . . . Thought I was going to die . . . This is why I hate summer.

AMY: lol. I never go shopping with my mom anymore for that exact reason. Guess you are learning . . .

ME: How was day "numero uno" of ballet camp?

AMY: day numero uno was "bien," thank you for asking. I missed you tho. I keep thinking how nice it would be if you were up here and dancing with me the whole time!

ME: I wish I was there too . . . Cant wait till you get back to NJ . . . But I bet you look hot in your little outfit thing, what's it called again?

AMY: You mean a TUTU?? I do look hot!

ME: That's so cool. but you always look hot . . .

AMY: ;-)

ME: literally just mowed the whole lawn . . . And not just the
back, but the front, you know where we have all those
stupid trees my mom likes? I had to do like figure eights
around them because my mom likes the pattern it makes
with the lawn mower. SO friggin' boring! I'm so tired . . .

AMY: hey you. ballet was awesome today. their making me the
lead in the "end of the summer" recital! which just means
I have to learn a lot of complicated solo parts, actually not
totally fun but a kind of nice thing, I guess, right??

ME: thats so cool!!! your gonna look so pretty in the show.
I can't wait to see it . . . But obviously I will wait, because it's not until the END of the summer. Which is I
guess why they call it an END OF THE SUMMER show,
right??

AMY: LOL! You are so funny.

ME: You are so pretty . . .

AMY: Well than I guess we make a Pretty Funny couple.

ME: LOL.

AMY: I really like you.

ME: I really like too . . .

ME: I mean I really like YOU too!

ME: Whoops . . .

AMY: what you doin' today?

ME: nothing . . . I kind of slept in which was weird because I
normally can't do that . . . So I woke up at like 2:30 and

was like "whoa" because I thought it was probably still morning . . . You?

AMY: we had our first rehearsal with costumes. mine looks SO nice, it's got these red sequins all over the back but it still moves really well. I'm supposed to be like a kind of bird, but a bird who does ballet (who knew?) and we met the costume guy who's this Brazilian guy I think. He's like the most beautiful man on the planet. He used to be a dancer. Don't get jealous. probably gay, everyone thinks so. And I have to wear this really short skirt and I told paolo (costume guy) that you can totally see my butt and he looked at me all serious and said with his awesome accent "you must be proud of your beautiful posterior." Wish he wasn't gay! Just kidding! Miss ya! Going out with Paolo and some of the gang to TGI Fridays for Sundays. (On Saturday. Weird. Almost covering all the days in one trip!)

ME: That dress sounds insane! Make sure you show off your "beautiful posterior" when I'm at the show! I had a really exciting day (he said sarcastically . . .) I helped my father at his office for like ten minutes and then was like going totally crazy, so I snuck out while he was with a patient. Anyway, back home now. Will probably watch a dumb movie or something . . . Can't wait for school to start! (and can't believe I actually just said that)

AMY: Just got home from dinner. On a sugar high. Will probably not sleep all night!

ME: how's it going? another boring day here . . . I wish I could hibernate like a bear does and just sleep through the whole summer and just wake up for when I get to SEE YOU AGAIN! I am GOING CRAZY at home . . . My parents are insane . . . They don't even fight like normal parents, its so annoying, they just get along and it's so boring. BUT . . .

Good news is (drum roll please): my sister Kendra gets back from college tomorrow!! She is so cool, I can't wait for you guys to meet. Maybe we could all hang out? She's super super smart, used to do all my history homework for me (dont tell Miss Matthews) and shes getting her degree in something totally random like the Bosnian genocide or something. Creepy! But whatever, can't wait to see her . . .

AMY: that sounds cool. I have some good news as well (second drum roll please): Paolo is NOT gay! LOL. Glad I didn't bet any money on that. Anyway, rehearsals are going really well. I'm working SO HARD, my body is getting like a crazy work out every single minute. But I think I'm doing really good and actually think I may be able to do this for a living. Like I used to think dancing was just a kid's dream kind of thing, but I actually think I might be good enough to do it for real. Weird!

ME: Yeah, that is weird . . . It's like if I was in the nba or something . . . Lol . . . But cool . . .

AMY: It's not like if you were in the nba. I mean I'm actually dancing and im the lead in the show. it would be like the nba if you were at a basketball camp and you were the best player and were also like really tall.

ME: im just saying, you should probably not like QUIT SCHOOL if that's what you were thinking . . . And I'm actually a really great long-range shooter. I was on JV last year and actually started some games, and you don't have to be tall if you have an outside shot, so . . .

AMY: I'm not quitting school! I'm just exploring who I am right now and I think I'm a really good dancer. Sorry if that pisses you off?

ME: I'm not pissed off? What? I'm just saying it might be a little EARLY to consider a career in a weird field . . . Sorry for being, like, practical . . . And Im glad paolo is not gay. Now you guys can be lovers . . . Honestly, though, be carful around those creepy old Brazilian guys!

AMY: Paolo is our age.

ME: What?

AMY: Yeah . . .

ME: And they let him design all the costumes?

AMY: He's a prodigy.

ME: Weird . . .

AMY: Why weird?

ME: Don't know . . . Just seems weird.

AMY: I feel like your being unsupportive.

ME: Well its a little hard to be supportive when your like changing your whole entire life around overnight with out telling me . . .

AMY: i didn't realize i had to tell you every time i move a muscle. I didn't realize we were like joined at the hip because we went on two dates before the summer

started. Sorry I didn't realize that! Anyway I have rehearsal. What exciting thing are you going to do? Wash
your socks?

ME: I'm actually hanging out with my sister. she's awesome
and we're probably gonna do something cool like go on a
trip to the beach or go to a party or something . . .

AMY: well have a good time. I'm actually going to a party also.
Paolo is having one at his room.

ME: have a good time . . .

AMY: Maybe I will!

ME: your being a bitch.

AMY: I think we should stop talking to each other.

ME: Good! How is that any different from our current
situation?

AMY: Good point for once!

ME: I've told my sister about what you're doing. She's going to
email you.

AMY: Fine! I didn't do anything wrong, so I don't care!

KENDRA: Dear Amy, this is Kendra. Nice to email meet you. :-)
My brother shared with me your recent email commu-
nications and, while I don't want to be invasive, I do feel
like I might be able to clarify my brother's position vis-
à-vis your new relationship and shed some light on the
situation.

AMY: Hi Kendra. Nice to email meet you too. ;-) I've been feeling so frustrated about the whole thing. Thanks for trying to help.

KENDRA: My pleasure. I'd like to share something with you

that I wish someone shared with me when I was your age. I think it might help illuminate some of the more complicated aspects of your relationship. The situation reminds me of a little historical blip called the Karađorđevo agreement. I imagine this may be a new reference for you so let me give you a little backstory.

In 1991, Bosnia, Serbia, and Croatia were preparing for war. Bosnia, led by the toothless Alija Izetbegović, was the weakest country and doomed to be overrun. Nonetheless, on March 25, 1991, the leaders of Croatia and Serbia met privately to discuss how they would carve up Bosnia. That's right. Behind the broken backs of the Bosnians, the Croatian and Serbian heads of state decided how Bosnia would be divided. Shocked? It gets worse.

Serbia, as you probably know, was represented by the vile Slobodan Milošević. Croatia was represented by the comparatively less ferocious President Franjo Tuđman. At Karađorđevo, these conspirators secretly agreed how they would overrun the helpless Izetbegović and his Bosnian Muslims and thus began a campaign of ethnic cleansing. I think, judging from your exchanges with my brother these past weeks, the Karađorđevo agreement is a fitting analogy to our situation. Let me explain the parallels, in case they don't seem immediately evident:

Clearly, my brother is Bosnian leader Alija Izetbegović, stuck in the dark while his fate is decided in private backroom deals by others: namely you and Paolo. Their crime? Not being present: Izetbegović, isolated in the boiling Sarajevan valley. My brother, mowing lawns in the suburbs of New Jersey.

While I am not equating you with Milošević (and I will get to him later), I do think your actions are reminiscent of Croatia's (weak) strongman Franjo Tuđman. He was, for all intents and purposes, a patsy. Was he evil? History will be the best judge, but I would say Not Necessarily. Still, he was certainly not innocent. Likely bullied by the stronger Milošević, Tuđman conspired as well, hatching the evil plot to carve up Bosnia. Whether you consider him an appeaser or a butcher, he certainly did nothing to help the poor Bosnians and nothing to stop the ruthless Milošević.

How do I think you are similar to Tuđman? Your increasingly intimate trysts with this Paolo character read like a crime of passivity. From ice cream sundaes at TGI Fridays to last night's party at "Paolo's room," you are carving Bosnia up one "innocent" interaction at a time. Just like Tuđman, you are complying with a plot that is far more complicated and evil than you are likely aware. Again, *you* are not evil. But lest we forget the famous words of Elie Wiesel: "To remain silent and indifferent is the greatest sin of all."

Now. On to Paolo, our Milošević. You call Paolo a "prodigy." And that may be true. Milošević was also a "prodigy." As were Mussolini and Hitler. And though you claim that Paolo's genius lies in the world of fashion, I think it is far closer to Milošević. That is, I think they are both experts not in fashion, but in butchery and thievery.

Questions of his sexuality aside, Paolo's intentions are clear. His comment about your "beautiful posterior" is tantamount to a declaration of war. Similarly, Milošević made no secret of his similarly dark intentions for the Bosnian Muslims, saying of the Karađorđevo accord: "It is a solution which is offering to the Muslims much more than they can ever dream to take by force."[1]

In summation, I am not blaming you and I am certainly not calling you evil, but I do feel like my brother is getting steamrolled and you are sitting silently in the passenger seat.

AMY: Dear Kendra, I understand your trying to help and that you think I'm not evil or whatever, but I completely disagree with you. And as long as we're "explaining" ourselves, let me explain MYSELF, okay? First of all, I read a little bit about the "Tudman" guy and I don't think I'm being like him at ALL. And, if anything, YOU GUYS are being like Milosevic, like conspiring against me in your dark ivory tower back in New Jersey. I'm literally just up here trying to focus on my dancing and I'm enjoying myself for the first time and feeling like I might be good at something and that's not a crime. If I WAS like a former Yugoslavian republic, then I'd be Slovenia, which I just looked up, because they were trying to get some independence without screwing anything up. And that's

---

1. John F. Burns, "Serbian Plan Would Deny the Muslims Any State," *New York Times*, July 18, 1993.

what I'm trying to do here at ballet camp, just have some fun and get some freedom without screwing up the relationship with your brother. And then YOU'RE BEING like Milosevic and the Yugoslav People's Army, storming Ljubljana with YPA troops as though what I'm doing is so bad.

And as for paolo, who I'm NOT defending: he is not as bad as Milosevic! That's not fair. He may be flirtatious, but that's just part of his *culture*. And nothing is happening between us. If anything, he's like former Speaker of the Croatian Parliament, President Stjepan Mesić: harmless.

KENDRA: *Harmless?* I am literally ROFL, Amy! Mesić was an Ustaše apologist(!) and a severely corrupt leader of an already corrupt state, with a shoddy presidential campaign bankrolled by the Albanian Mafia! Maybe if you did less dancing in your little bird costume (hope PETA doesn't come to the show!) and more studying about Central European post-Soviet conflict zones, you would know what you were talking about!

AMY: First of all, I'm a vegan (unlike your saintly/victimized little brother) so don't get me started about PETA. Second of all, Mesić was never convicted of any corruption charges related to his campaign, so don't go throwing around accusations like their convictions.[2]

KENDRA: Apologies for my tangential comments about your

---

2. "Sud: Darko Petričić nije oklevetao Stjepana Mesića," *Slobodna Dalmacija*, March 29, 2012.

bird costume. It actually sounds nice (I love sequins on anything!) and I commend you for your vegan lifestyle, which is a diet I support but struggle to personally implement.

AMY: Thanks for your apology re: my costume (I love sequens too!!!) As for your diet, you should try quinoia with a light soy sauce, unless you're gluten free?

KENDRA: No, I'm not gluten free (anymore!). I was for like three months. Lost eight pounds! Then found it again. ;-(

AMY: Hate that! ANYWAY. Regarding Paolo, yes I am spending time with him and YES, I think he's attractive, but that doesn't mean I'm like cheating on your brother, who by the way, would do the SAME THING, if the roles were reversed. Like if Radovan Karadžić had gone to school in Škofja Loka and Jože Pučnik in Banja Luka—I don't think Jože would exactly be walking around Eurozone meetings right now giving double cheek kisses to Christine Lagarde! What would Slavoj Žižek say about your moral absolutism?

KENDRA: Hmm. Žižek would probably be unimpressed with my impractical strivings for a false post-Marxist utopia.

AMY: And another thing! If you think Alija Izetbegović was a benign victim maybe you should read his 1970 manifesto *Islamic Declaration*, which I just downloaded in PDF. It has eerily similar passages to emails that your brother has sent me—Izetbegović calling for the modernization of Bosnia *only* in conjunction with the teachings of the Qur'an and your brother calling for me to meet him after school *only* if I agree to bowling (which

I hate doing and which he knows because it hurts my
thumbs!)

KENDRA: Dear Amy, your points are insightful, valid, and ultimately well researched. (I did not know about the
bowling incident.) In light of these sobering thoughts, I
actually do think a breakup between you and my brother,
not dissimilar to the former Yugoslavia, is coming. While
I would love to see you two stay together, the world knew
that, without Tito, Yugoslavia would never maintain
stability and, without real understanding, you and my
brother are likely doomed. And, in an attempt to avoid
another Srebrenića, I think a peaceful breakup would be
best.

Frankly, the last thing I would want to do is what the
United States did under Clinton, which we both know
was too little and too late. In that way, I think that maybe
you and my brother should part ways before the fighting
becomes even more violent than it already is. I wish you
the best with your upcoming recital and I will relay our
decision to my brother, who will most likely not attend it
now that you two are no longer together.

AMY: Dear Kendra, thank you for your sensitive remarks
and for not being a bitch like I was worried you might
be. I look forward to meeting you in person ;-) even if it
means going behind your brothers back (Karadơorđevo
Round 2? JK). Although, just to make sure things don't
get too heated, we should probably meet with a media-
tor like former Assistant Secretary of State Richard Hol-
brooke! lol!

KENDRA: Right! Or Slovak diplomat Miroslav Lajčák! So we don't wind up with another Višegrad!

AMY: Or worse, Foča!

KENDRA: LMFAO!

AMY: ;-) Have a great summer Kendra.

KENDRA: You too.

MY PRESCRIPTION INFORMATION PAMPHLETS AS WRITTEN BY MY FATHER

BRAND NAME: Ativan

GENERIC NAME: Lorazepam (*lor-A-ze-pam*)

CLASS: Anti-anxiety/Sleep Aid

COMMON USE: This medication was prescribed by your doctor to help you sleep because it's difficult to fall asleep when you don't engage in physical activity.

SIDE EFFECTS: May cause fatigue, though this probably won't affect your schedule.

IN CASE OF OVERDOSE: Drink several ounces of water, which comes out of the faucet and could also be used to wash dishes.

BRAND NAME: Adderall

GENERIC NAME: Amphetamine and Dextroamphetamine (*am-FET-a-meen and DEX-troe-am-FET-a-meen*)

CLASS: Stimulant

COMMON USE: This medication was overprescribed by your doctor because he's paid by the pharmaceutical industry to overprescribe this to you. Do you know how many people were on Adderall in the last four years? Thirty-seven million! That's two million more people than the entire population of Canada—a country that, not incidentally, banned Adderall! It's legal to smoke Marijuana in Canada (and I know you have; your sister told me that you smoked Marijuana with your friend Peter Jaworski when he was at McGill), but Adderall is illegal!

SIDE EFFECTS: May be habit forming. In the same way lateness, dressing like a teenager, and not sending your mother birthday cards has become habit forming.

IN CASE OF OVERDOSE: Taking any amount of this medication is an overdose.

BRAND NAME: Zoloft

GENERIC NAME: Sertraline (*SER-tra-leen*)

CLASS: Antidepressant/Selective Serotonin Reuptake Inhibitor

COMMON USE: This medication was prescribed by your doctor because you probably told him about the time I threw the alarm clock at the wall and accidentally hit you in the head. I was throwing it AT THE WALL! I had a terrible day; a man is allowed to throw things in his own home. I have apologized that it accidentally hit you in the head—a fact I don't dispute—but you should apologize for this constant, frankly self-aggrandizing and self-pitying claim of child abuse that never existed. You're not happy? Who's happy? Why does everyone in this country think a pill will make them happy? Did you know that China is now producing more doctors and engineers than the United States? And what are you doing about it? You're writing a book! Wow! Thank you! Thank you, son, for writing an "ironic" book about talking chimpanzees in New York City! If it's as "meta" and "reflexive" as you claim, it will probably bring us out of this recession! Take that, China and India! A "postmodern" book about talking monkeys!

SIDE EFFECTS: This medication causes severe erectile dysfunction. And beyond any concern for your tawdry sex life, your mother would like grandchildren at some point and, with your sister currently gay, you're the last Mohican.

IN CASE OF OVERDOSE: Stick your finger down your throat and stand over the toilet. And don't just run into the kitchen and throw up in front of your mother like you "couldn't make it to the bathroom in time." Everyone knows that's a bullshit ploy for sympathy. But it doesn't work. It just makes her nauseous.

BRAND NAME: Haldol

GENERIC NAME: Haloperidol (*HAL-oh-PER-i-dol*)

CLASS: Antipsychotic/Schizophrenia (Jesus Christ!)

COMMON USE: Are you selling this on the street or something? How did you even get it? Did you tell your psychiatrist you hear voices or something? Well, hear this: If you want me to keep paying for your COBRA so you can pay this shrink, you need to get a job. How could you even trust a doctor like this? Who the hell is this guy? I told you to come home to New Jersey, don't go to a shrink in the West Village. Your mother and I are right by the university. The doctors there are just fine and they're half the price. You know, Howard asked me about you the other day and I accidentally told him you were taking this Haldol drug. It's embarrassing to me. None of his kids take anything like this and Jenny's dyslexic.

SIDE EFFECTS: It's probably too bad I was never prescribed these pick-me-ups when I was abusing my gay, schizophrenic children. I was probably too busy heaving alarm clocks at your head to indulge in a hoity-toity, West Village, $350-a-minute shoulder to cry on! And I turned out terribly, didn't I?! Becoming the youngest partner at my firm! Buying a six-bedroom, three-and-a-half-bath in Fort Lee! Twenty-six years married to the same woman and three Carnival Cruises together! Yeah, I'm a really awful person.

IN CASE OF OVERDOSE: Don't tell your mother.

MY NEPHEW HAS
SOME QUESTIONS

ME: I need you to buckle up back there, buddy.

MY NEPHEW: Why?

ME: I just do.

MY NEPHEW: Why?

ME: Because I care about you.

MY NEPHEW: Why?

ME: Because you're my sister's son. And I care about her.

MY NEPHEW: Why?

ME: Because I just do.

MY NEPHEW: Why?

ME: Because, I guess, when I was born, she was three years old, and like any younger sibling I put her on a pedestal.

MY NEPHEW: Why?

ME: I probably idealized her, which is strange considering your mom was not very nice to me.

MY NEPHEW: Why?

ME: She was an only child and when I came along she was forced to share everything.

MY NEPHEW: Why?

ME: We both had needs and I think it was difficult for our parents to satisfy us both.

MY NEPHEW: Why?

ME: Because needs are so ephemeral. I think it was Maslow who said, "It's a rare and difficult psychological achievement to know what we want."

MY NEPHEW: Why?

ME: Because he was writing at a time when social psychology was bending toward humanism and self-actualization.

MY NEPHEW: Why?

ME: Because there was this trend in post-Freudian behavior study that was vastly underexamined in Western psychology.

MY NEPHEW: Why?

ME: Because the world was still sorting everything out. Well, not the whole world. The East, in its way, had already found answers.

MY NEPHEW: Why?

ME: Because their societies were more fixed.

MY NEPHEW: Why?

ME: Probably because of the Mongols. They unified these huge swaths of cultures by force.

MY NEPHEW: Why?

ME: I guess they thought that amassing land was important.

MY NEPHEW: Why?

ME: Because it was the most explicit form of achievement. Today, we value amassing currency.

MY NEPHEW: Why?

ME: Because it's easier than invading a country. But in some ways it could be just as dangerous—if not more.

MY NEPHEW: Why?

ME: Because there's a finite amount of land. But currency expands exponentially.

MY NEPHEW: Why?

ME: Partly due to the nature of economy, but also because of some ill-conceived relationships between the developing world and economic organizations—the World Bank, the IMF. Look at Zimbabwe.

MY NEPHEW: Why?

ME: Because it's a good example of how inflation can ravage a country. People were literally taking wheelbarrows of cash to buy a loaf of bread.

MY NEPHEW: Why?

ME: Because there was a power-hungry dictator promoting failed land reform policies.

MY NEPHEW: Why?

ME: Because for so long it had been a white colony—Rhodesia—with generations of horrible disenfranchisement.

MY NEPHEW: Why?

ME: Because there was a scramble for power. (Which goes back to what we were saying about the Mongols.)

MY NEPHEW: Why?

ME: It's the nature of man. And, I guess, in some ways, *I'm* a victim of this unquenchable thirst for money.

MY NEPHEW: Why?

ME: Well, it's easy to blame the "system"—capitalism, pioneer culture in the United States, what Chomsky called "economic fascism"—but it's probably my own fault.

MY NEPHEW: Why?

ME: Because I had opportunities to take a different path, but for some reason, I felt compelled to chase the elusive dollar. You know, I actually wanted to be a philosophy major.

MY NEPHEW: Why?

ME: It's totally corny, but as a teenager I loved Immanuel Kant.

MY NEPHEW: Why?

ME: No one's ever asked me that before, little guy. But I guess I loved how *simple* he made everything.

MY NEPHEW: Why?

ME: Because Kant gave concrete answers to complicated problems and that was comforting.

MY NEPHEW: Why?

ME: Because I had tons of questions about morality and ethics.

MY NEPHEW: Why?

ME: You know, I haven't talked about this in years, but I spent some time in a juvenile detention center when I was twelve.

MY NEPHEW: Why?

ME: Because they accused me of breaking into school in the middle of the night and setting one of the classrooms on fire.

MY NEPHEW: Why?

ME: Because my parents reported me missing that night and the classroom that was set on fire was my math classroom. And it was the night after a big math test. So I seemed like the obvious suspect.

MY NEPHEW: Why?

ME: Because everything pointed to me. But I didn't do it!

MY NEPHEW: Why?

ME: Because I didn't care if I failed that test!

MY NEPHEW: Why?

ME: Because it's not like if I got a bad grade on that math test, then I wouldn't get into a good college and wouldn't get a good job and I would die penniless and starving!

MY NEPHEW: Why?

ME: Okay! I did it! I burned down that classroom!

MY NEPHEW: Why?

ME: Because I was panicked. And I was *twelve*! I made a mistake!

MY NEPHEW: Why?

ME: Because I'm human! I'm fallible! I just wanted to be loved!

MY NEPHEW: Why?

ME: Because we live in this crazy world where we have to

fight for every scrap, and I'm constantly scared that if I slow down, the world is just gonna pass me by. Everything moves so quickly, so chaotically, so uncaringly fast, threatening at all times to mow us down or overtake us. And so I speed up too! I join the rat race! I know it's unhealthy, I know it's wrong, but I can't slow down! It's why I burned down that school! It's why I blame everything on the Mongols and the World Bank and the IMF and Robert Mugabe and Cecil Rhodes and Immanuel Kant and Freud and Maslow and Chomsky and your mother! But it's *me*. It's just me! *That's* why I wanted you to strap in! I wanted you to strap in because I don't trust myself to slow down enough to avoid an accident. The "seat belt" is just a frail bandage on my reckless life!

MY NEPHEW: Why?

ME: Because I'm damaged. I'm in pain! And I'm not gonna get better. Not without real help. So can you strap in? Just for now?

MY NEPHEW: Okay.

ME: Thanks, little buddy. Thanks a lot.

III.
HISTORY

MEN AND DANCING

NATIVE AMERICAN WOMAN: Your people are starving! There has
been no rain! The crops cannot grow!

NATIVE AMERICAN MAN: The rain gods have ignored all my pleas.

WOMAN: It's because you are not appealing to the gods in the
right way.

MAN: I was going to sacrifice another sheep but you get skit-
tish around blood.

WOMAN: We don't need another dead sheep, the only solution
to our famine is the sacred rain dance.

MAN: The *only* solution?

WOMAN: Yes, you must do a rain dance or we'll all starve to
death.

MAN: Okay, I'll just go into the woods and do the dance.

WOMAN: No, in order to appeal to the rain gods, you must dance in front of the whole tribe, while we point and laugh at you, as is our native custom.

MAN: You know who's actually a really good dancer? Two Dogs Prancing Unselfconsciously Across New Horizon. Two Dogs could probably do a great rain dance.

WOMAN: No, it must be you.

MAN: And what about bear meat? I can go hunt some more bears.

WOMAN: We have enough bear meat for ten moon cycles. What we need is rain!

MAN: And I hear that. I totally hear you. Listen: You wait here. I'm just going to go to the forest, make sure there aren't any other bears, check in with Two Dogs, and I'll be right back to do the dancing thing.

KING'S AIDE: The king requests a performance.

JESTER: Great. What's he looking for this time? I could do my bit about the moat.

KING'S AIDE: No, the king would like to see a dance.

JESTER: Are you sure? He loves moat jokes. You know: What do you call a moat in winter? Useless. Get it?

KING'S AIDE: Yeah, 'cause it's frozen.

JESTER: Or: How many alligators does it take to stop an invading Hun? Thirty-one. One to kill the Hun and another thirty to get rid of the stench.

KING'S AIDE: Right, because Huns smell bad. I get it. But that's

not gonna work this time. The king demands
a dance.

JESTER: And what happens if I don't do the dance?

KING'S AIDE: If you don't dance, His Highness has requested
that your body be slowly torn apart for his amusement.

JESTER: I see.

KING'S AIDE: Yes, it would be a slow but hilarious death.

JESTER: Right . . . Maybe I'll *open* with the moat bit.

PROTESTOR 1: Hey, brother, you ready for the big protest?

PROTESTOR 2: Absolutely! What's the plan?

PROTESTOR 1: We're all gonna take LSD and protest the Vietnam War on the Washington Mall.

PROTESTOR 2: Great! Finally those bastards in Washington will learn that the way we're imposing our hege-
monic capitalist ideology on this poor Asian country is
reprehensible.

PROTESTOR 1: Exactly! So just pop some LSD under that tongue
so we can get to dancing.

PROTESTOR 2: Excuse me?

PROTESTOR 1: You're not scared of a little LSD, are you?

PROTESTOR 2: No! Not at all. I'm totally good with LSD. But did
you say dancing?

PROTESTOR 1: Yeah. That's our protest. Just let our bodies loose
on the Washington Mall, flailing them around freely in
opposition to the war.

PROTESTOR 2: Oh. That sounds fun, really. But, just to play

devil's advocate, do you really feel we've exhausted all of our options? Have you considered making signs?

PROTESTOR 1: None of that stuff works! What we need to send a message to those hawks in DC is some good old-fashioned, unselfconscious dancing.

PROTESTOR 2: Right, sure. But have you considered all sides of the war? I mean it's not so clean-cut. Aren't you worried about the domino effect?

PROTESTOR 1: The domino effect?

PROTESTOR 2: Yeah. Say we get out of Vietnam, everyone goes home, a tiny country turns communist, no big deal. But then Laos goes communist, then Indonesia and China, and suddenly Karl Marx is knocking on your door, handing you a red book and asking you to work in his shoe factory.

QUARTERBACK: Great catch, rookie! Your first touchdown! Now do your thing!

WIDE RECEIVER: My thing? What do you mean?

QUARTERBACK: Your dance.

WIDE RECEIVER: Oh . . . I don't do that.

QUARTERBACK: When you score a touchdown, you have to do a dance.

TIGHT END: Yeah, we all do it.

RUNNING BACK: I rehearsed mine this morning just in case I got a touchdown.

WIDE RECEIVER: You *rehearsed*?

running back: Of course. All of our dances have complicated moves.

tight end: And even though they're different dances, what unifies them is our complete lack of self-consciousness.

wide receiver: I guess I always thought it was optional.

running back: No, it's mandatory. Especially because this game is nationally televised.

tight end: Right, so all the girls from your high school are watching.

running back: Yes, and Seth Neddermeyer, who bullied you before your growth spurt. He's going to watch you dance too.

wide receiver: Maybe I could just spike the ball or something.

offensive lineman: I just dislocated my shoulder for you! Do your dance!

wide receiver: Can I do a moonwalk? Are people still doing the moonwalk?

quarterback: No, you have to do an *original* dance.

wide receiver: You know, I think my foot may have been on the line. I think I may have stepped out near the twenty. Maybe we should check the replay.

FINAL CONVERSATIONS
AT POMPEII

MISTRESS: Stop! Get off me!

MAN: What's wrong?

MISTRESS: I can't keep doing this!

MAN: This always happens just as you're about to have a feeling.

MISTRESS: It just feels so dirty. Meeting here every week.

MAN: Dirty?! This is one of the nicest villas in Vesuvius's shadow!

MISTRESS: And I keep having this fear that someone is going to find out about us.

MAN: What are you talking about? This place is half empty. You know all the Samnites go to the Sarno this time of year.

MISTRESS: You would never take me to the Sarno.

MAN: You live in a different hamlet! It's a six-day walk not including stops for cattle castration!

MISTRESS: But you would take your wife there.

MAN: Don't make this about Debbie.

MISTRESS: You said you would tell her about me.

MAN: And I will! It's just not the right time.

MISTRESS: So when is the right time? Six months from now? A year?!

MAN: Can't we just enjoy each other? We have such little time together.

MISTRESS: How can I enjoy myself when she could walk in on us at any minute?

MAN: Relax. We are totally alone. In a thousand years, no one would ever walk in here.

ARTIST: I've been stuck in a rut.

MUSE: What are you talking about? You're at the top of your game.

ARTIST: I haven't been able to do anything in months.

MUSE: You just did that great fresco with the cattle and the phallus. Everyone loved that.

ARTIST: No one even saw it. At this rate, I couldn't even get a gallery show in Umbria.

MUSE: Are you jealous of Augusto?

ARTIST: This is not about Augusto. This is about me and my inertia.

MUSE: Don't forget how much everyone loved your grape
sculpture.

ARTIST: That was like three years ago.

MUSE: But it was ahead of its time! Who else would've thought
to use lamb's brain for texture?

ARTIST: (*scoffs*) Certainly not Augusto.

MUSE: That's right! You're a pioneer!

ARTIST: Augusto probably would've used eunuch's liver.

MUSE: So obvious.

ARTIST: Or calf's ear.

MUSE: So passé.

ARTIST: I feel like I was born in the wrong millennium. I feel
like people can't appreciate me now.

MUSE: That's what I've been saying! You're a progressive refor-
mationist stuck in the counter-reformation.

ARTIST: My stuff is too radical for the counter-reformation!

MUSE: In a thousand years, this place will be a museum.

ARTIST: You really think so?

MUSE: Absolutely. People will come from all over just to see
your work. They'll cross land bridges! They'll seize ships
at Aden just to see those lamb's brain grapes. You'll make
Pompeii famous.

ARTIST: And Augusto will still be working downtown
Nuceria!

MUSE: Exactly! But don't make this about Augusto.

PRISONER 1: Hey, man, wake up. We're bustin' outta here.

PRISONER 2: What?

PRISONER 1: Warden's kid got the plague. Coast is clear. Don't tell me you're gettin' cold feet.

PRISONER 2: I'm actually thinkin' I might stay.

PRISONER 1: You wanna stay in prison?

PRISONER 2: We only got three months left anyway. We should just pay our debt to society; I mean, we really shouldn't have tipped over those goats.

PRISONER 1: You sayin' you like it here?

PRISONER 2: I kind of do. I've met some nice people and I have a good job in the prison library, looking after the books.

PRISONER 1: Well, I'm gettin' outta here. Tonight!

PRISONER 2: But you'll spend the rest of your life in Pompeii looking over your shoulder.

PRISONER 1: No, I'm bouncin' outta Pompeii altogether.

PRISONER 2: You're gonna leave Pompeii?

PRISONER 1: I'm sick of it here. I have dreams, man. I wanna travel up the coast, fall in love with a Babylonian woman, and then stone her to death when she menstruates.

PRISONER 2: That does sound nice. But I think I prefer to serve out my time here and live a relaxing life in Pompeii. Maybe teach Latin to at-risk youth. You know, give back a little.

PRISONER 1: Well, it was nice knowing you, brother.

PRISONER 2: See ya on the outside.

WIFE: Can you please sit still?

HUSBAND: I am.

WIFE: No, you keep sneaking little looks into your telescope.

HUSBAND: I'm just checking to make sure the kids are in bed.

WIFE: No, I see you peering over the valley. You're checking on the game.

HUSBAND: Well, the bear mauling finals started tonight.

WIFE: And you can check the score as soon as we get home. Please just pay attention.

HUSBAND: I'm trying, but this is literally my worst nightmare, being stuck watching a three-hour performance of guys prancing around in satyr suits.

WIFE: Your worst nightmare is being stuck with me?

HUSBAND: No! I love being with you. I was referring to the satyrs. But is this whole thing gonna be in Oscan? I can't understand a word they're saying.

WIFE: Claudius takes his wife to hymn cantations every week.

HUSBAND: So maybe you should go with them.

WIFE: And be a third wheel like on an oxen-pulled cart? No thank you!

HUSBAND: I feel like this thing is never going to end.

WIFE: Just be glad we're not at Flaccus's pantomime. It'll all be over in three hours.

METEOROLOGIST 1: Have you noticed anything strange recently?

METEOROLOGIST 2: Strange?

METEOROLOGIST 1: Yeah, I don't know. Just feels like the weather's been eerily calm.

METEOROLOGIST 2: Well, what's the forecast for the weekend? Have you checked your leaf?

METEOROLOGIST 1: Yeah, it's still blowing toward Capri.

METEOROLOGIST 2: So we're fine. You're probably feeling pressure from Titus to invent some crazy story just to boost ratings.

METEOROLOGIST 1: No, come on. I wouldn't do that.

METEOROLOGIST 2: I'm not saying you're doing it intentionally. But remember last year, when you said frogs would fall from sky? You always do this during sweeps.

METEOROLOGIST 1: Do I?

METEOROLOGIST 2: Yes! We're fine! Look! The sun is shining. We're in Pompeii, the safest hamlet this side of Herculaneum!

METEOROLOGIST 1: Maybe you're right.

METEOROLOGIST 2: Of course I'm right.

METEOROLOGIST 1: I sometimes have this fantasy of running into the amphitheater and telling everyone to evacuate Pompeii, that there's some crazy flood of ashen pumice about to shoot out of the sky, paralyzing us all!

METEOROLOGIST 2: You'd probably get an 8 or 9 share in the ratings.

METEOROLOGIST 1: At least an 8 or 9!

METEOROLOGIST 2: But would it be the right thing to do?

METEOROLOGIST 1: I guess not.

METEOROLOGIST 2: Good. Now let's kick back, grab some fermented goat tonic, and watch the sun set behind placid Mount Vesuvius.

ALEXANDER GRAHAM BELL'S FIRST FIVE PHONE CALLS

March 10, 1876

ALEXANDER GRAHAM BELL: Watson, come here! I want to see you!

March 11, 1876

ALEXANDER GRAHAM BELL: Hey, Watson, *guess who*? Yeah, it's me, it's Aleck. How'd you know? But I was doing a funny voice! Did you get any sleep last night? Me neither! I was so pumped about the whole phone thing working. I know! I totally wanted to call you too, but I figured you probably went to sleep. Did you tell anybody yet? No, me neither. I was thinking of telling Mabel though. I bet she would think it was interesting. All right, cool. If you're up later, though, call me. I don't care what time it is. Cool.

So . . . are you gonna hang up? No, you hang up first. No, *you*! Okay, we'll do it at the same time. Ready? On three. One. Two. Three. Are you still there? Yeah, me too. Okay, I'm really hanging up this time. One. Two. Three. Hello?

March 12, 1876

ALEXANDER GRAHAM BELL: Hey, Watson, how's it going? Nothing. Just sitting here. You? That's cool. Hey, I had a kind of weird idea. Tell me if it sounds too creepy. You know how you have a phone and I have a phone? Don't you think it would be cool if more people had one? I don't know, like Mabel for instance. I just think she would like it. What? No, I don't like her, I just think she would like the phone. I'm not *obsessed* with her. I just think it would be a cool experiment, to see if it could work at her house. So I was thinking we could make it a surprise, you know? Like you could hide the phone in her house and then I could call her and she'll hear it ringing and not know what it is and then pick up and I'll be on the other end and I'll say something really casual like, "Hey, Mabel, it's me Aleck calling from my house down the block," and she'll be so impressed—not that I'm trying to impress her—and then we'll know it worked. So I was thinking if you could go to her house and sneak the phone in, that would be great. Like you could just casually knock on her door and pretend you're delivering flowers or something. Or doing a survey on plague in the neighborhood—just something totally casual. But don't mention me at all! Cool, thanks, Watson. You're the best! She's gonna be so impressed.

What? No, I mean with the *invention*. She's gonna be impressed with the *invention*. Cool, speak later.

March 15, 1876

ALEXANDER GRAHAM BELL: Hey, it's me. Nothing. What? No, I just ate dinner. I'm not slurring my words. I'm not. Well, I think *you're* drunk! I'm totally fine. I may have had a sip of wine, so what? Shut up! I'm not in the mood for this, okay? Have you heard anything from Mabel? I've been calling her all day, she doesn't pick up! Yes, of course I dialed the right number—2! Don't patronize me! You probably didn't connect the reeds to the armature properly. I'm not saying you did it on purpose, but it does seem a little odd that she hasn't picked up. That's all I'm saying. I'm not accusing you of anything, but I have seen the way you look at her. Oh, I'm just inventing things, am I?! The Great Inventor! Inventing things, right?! Like when you told her you liked her frock? Did I invent that? Or when you walked *curbside* with her all the way to Strawbridges?! Maybe I should get a patent on that vision! Ah! Now I feel enraged! I feel like hanging up my phone before we finish speaking to each other. I mean it! I'm going to do it. I'm going to hang up my phone even though we're not done!

March 21, 1876

ALEXANDER GRAHAM BELL: Hey, Watson, it's Aleck. How's it going? I'm okay. So . . . Yeah, I guess I just wanted to say sorry for my phone call last week. I should never have called you drunk. That was stupid. And I guess I wasn't really mad at you. I guess I was just . . . mad at the *situation*, you know? And I took it out on you, which was totally juvenile. Yeah, so anyway . . . How are you? That's good, that's good. Yeah, no otherwise, I'm pretty good too. I thought I had an idea for a new invention but I think someone already did it. It was like a spoon with ridges. Whatever. It's kind of stupid anyway. No, I haven't heard from Mabel. I don't even really like her that much. She's kind of self-involved, you know? Like she turns every conversation into something about herself. I think I was just in love with the *idea* of her, you know? Anyway, I am actually a little lonely. I do sound depressed, don't I? Watson, do you think you could come over here? I want to see you.

MARXIST-SOCIALIST JOKES

Why did the Marxist-Socialist cross the road?
To get to the Marxist-Socialist sit-in on the other side of the
road.

How many Marxist-Socialists does it take to screw in a
lightbulb?
Two. One to screw in the lightbulb, one to lament Milton
Friedman's laissez-faire economic policies.

A Marxist-Socialist walks into a bar and asks the bartender if
he's unionized.

Knock knock.
Who's there?

A Marxist-Socialist.

A Marxist-Socialist who?

A Marxist-Socialist who wants to give you a pamphlet about class struggle.

What did one Marxist-Socialist say to another?

Like you, I also advocate a proletarian revolution culminating in collective ownership.

What do you get when you cross a Marxist with a Socialist?

Two people who generally feel that the value of a commodity is equal to its socially necessary labor time.

What's the difference between a Marxist-Socialist and a Keynesian economist?

Several things, including but not limited to the following: The Marxist-Socialist believes that workers should own the means of production, whereas a Keynesian supports the private ownership of the means of production. The Marxist-Socialist believes that centralized government would ultimately wither away after a revolution, whereas the Keynesian advocates greater government action to ensure full societal employment. Finally, a Marxist-Socialist would not be invited to a party that a Keynesian was giving at work because the Keynesian knows that the Marxist-Socialist would throw a stink about the way the cubicles in the Keynesian's office were arranged.

How do you get a one-armed Marxist-Socialist out of a tree?

Ask two teamsters to drive three AFL-CIO riggers each carrying an IAFF-approved ladder to the tree and help the one-armed Marxist-Socialist down.

The Marxist-Socialist's mother is so fat that when the Marxist-Socialist's mother laments stagflation, she *actually* stagflates.

A Priest, a Rabbi, and a Marxist-Socialist are in an airplane that is going to crash and there are only two parachutes. The Priest says, "I have always followed the word of Jesus, so I should have one of the parachutes." The Rabbi says, "I paid for the plane rental, so I should also have one of the parachutes." The Marxist-Socialist says, "I would normally advocate allocating these out according to one's means, but I'm afraid of dying and would like one of the chutes, please."

IV.
MY ROOMMATE STOLE MY RAMEN

LETTERS FROM

A FRUSTRATED

FRESHMAN

September 16

Dear Miss Rita,

I bet you thought you'd never hear from me again, right? Well, here I am! I know we haven't spoken since my junior year of high school[1] but I am *so* distraught and you're the only person I could turn to. Oh, I should probably also tell you that I'm taking a creative writing class and we're learning how to use footnotes,[2] and I was writing so much to you that I thought it would be better if I used footnotes to make some of my points.

---

1. So technically you're not my guidance counselor anymore.
2. Which are these!

Okay, so back to what I was saying. I've been in college for two weeks now and it's been the worst time in my life. I am so unbelievably depressed! Even more than junior year, if you can believe that!

And I know writing to you is a totally random thing to do and you're probably thinking, "Who the hell is this?" but if I don't tell someone about what's going on, I think my head will explode.[3]

So, I didn't tell you, but I didn't get into any of my top schools *and* most of my safeties so I'm going to a school in The Middle of Fucking Nowhere, Missouri,[4] because my parents thought it would be "good for me" to leave home and "experience a different part of the country."[5]

And I hate this fucking town with a passion. It's literally like the United States government made a regular town and then took a shit on it. It's hard to describe, but St. Louis looks like shit, like actual feces, like there is a thin layer of excrement spread over everything in this town and that its heyday was like forty years ago, during the Depression era,[6] and I miss New York so much right now!

And the weirdest part about this whole thing is that I seem like the only one who actually minds this place. Every other student—and I mean *every* other student—seems totally fine. Like they're doing well in their classes and going out and

---

3. Literally. I'm actually having stress migraines.
4. Or, as Missouri calls it, St. Louis.
5. The shitty part, I guess.
6. There is literally a bowling alley here. I'm not kidding.

smiling and making friends and I'm just like, "How does any-one not see what a miserable fucking situation we're all in?!"

But the absolute worst part of my experience so far is that I requested a single room,[7] but there were only a few singles and I got stuck with a bitch of a roommate named Rebecca Slotnick.[8]

The Slutnick is *technically* a "nice" person. Like she always says the "right" things,[9] I guess, but it feels totally fake. It feels like she's only being nice so that, if we got into a fight, she could be like, "But I *asked* you if my music was bothering you." And then I would have no choice but to be like, "Yeah, I guess you did."

And, not that it's my business, but honestly, she should take up an eating disorder if she doesn't already have one be-cause she is a fucking chubster and a half.

Okay, so this brings me to my current complaint:

I did a massive shopping at Costco on move-in day with my parents cause I'm not allowed to have a car freshman year so we bought everything I would need for a few weeks.[10]

---

7. Which means no roommate. Which I wanted because I've never shared a room with anybody (not even like sleepovers, which you may remember I *don't* do).
8. Who I will heretofore refer to as The Slutnick and I'm sorry that it's rude to do that and maybe that word is offensive to you, but it makes me feel better to call her that so, sorry, Miss Rita. ;)
9. "I noticed you were reading, is my music bothering you?"
10. Including like four huge bottles of Pantene Pro-V shampoo and conditioner, tons of Ziploc bags, meds like DayQuil/NyQuil

cont.

And we bought an eighteen-pack of ramen noodles,[11] which I know are supposed to be bad for you, but I actually like them and they're the perfect "I have nothing else to eat!" kind of food.

And The Slutnick and I have different class schedules, so one day I was at class till like 8:30 at night and when I came back home, Slutnick's not there and I put a mug of water in the microwave to boil it for ramen. And then I take a bowl out and notice that there are only three chicken ramens left, when I distinctly remember there being four.

At first I thought there'd been a break-in or something. So I inspected the rest of the room, but nothing else seemed different. And then I realized that The Slutnick doesn't have class till late on Tuesdays so she's probably been in the room all day, just eating her dumb face off, and she probably got tempted by my chicken ramen and decided she needed to force that down her hole as well.

When I realized The Slutnick stole my ramen, I immediately lost my appetite. And something inside me kind of broke apart. Like when a woman finds out that her dentist husband has been cheating with his hygienist.

And I started to have those panic attack feelings that you described. Where my breathing is really quick but I also feel

---

(capsules), a mini-microwave, ultra-thin hangers, lemon-lime Gatorades, school supplies (notepads, binders, etc.). I'm sure I'm leaving like a million things out, but you get the idea. *Basic* stuff.
11. The kind in the styro bowls that comes with 6 bowls of shrimp, 6 bowls of beef, and 6 bowls of chicken.

like I'm choking. And my head feels dizzy and my toes feel empty like when I'm standing on the ledge of a tall building, looking down.

So I just sat on the bed and I actually started crying.[12] And I buried my head in the pillow and snot was just pouring out of my nose[13] and I started to really hate everything in the world and it felt like my life was actually over, like I was stuck in an impossible situation and that my life was going to end. My heart was beating so fast but I felt like I was dying.

And I guess I finally fell asleep, because the next thing I remember is Slutnick coming in the room and saying, "Hi, hope I didn't wake you up."[14]

And I kind of ignored her for a while and pretended to read. And then, at some point, I said, "Night," really quickly, to kind of show her that I was mad, and turned my lamp off and went to sleep.

BUT . . .

The next fucking day, Miss Rita . . .

. . . The Slutnick mentions the Ramen! And she did it in her classic phony way. She said, "I hope you don't mind, I was totally starved[15] yesterday and I had one of your Ramens."

I wanted to scream in her dumb frizzy face!

---

12. I know that's maybe weird to do, but I couldn't help it.
13. I would normally be disgusted by getting snot on the pillow, especially because it's a pain to do laundry here, but I couldn't stop crying.
14. I was thinking, "YOU DID WAKE ME UP!"
15. Irony alert, fatty!

First of all, no one should ever say, "I hope you don't mind." If you're saying "I hope you don't mind" then that usually means that the person you're saying it to DEFINITELY FUCKING MINDS.

Second of all, she didn't have "one" of my ramens. She had a *chicken* ramen. [16] That's like taking a hundred-dollar bill out of my wallet and saying, "I hope you don't mind, I took one of your bills."

And Third Of All, EAT SOME OF YOUR OWN FUCK-ING FOOD, BITCH! The Slutnick could've gone to Costco with her fat fucks of a family and she has tons of food on her side of the room.[17] So what would possess her fat fucking ass to waddle over to MY side of the room and rummage her pig fucking nose through my shit!?!? Stay on your own side of the fucking PEN, PIGGY!!! Oink oink! Oink all you want on YOUR SIDE you fat slutty bitch!!!

And then I told the fucking Resident Assistant on my floor[18] that The Slutnick took one of my Ramens and do you know what she said? She said: "I know college is a big transition for you, being an only child,[19] but you're going to have to

---

16. Everyone knows that the chicken is the only one that tastes good. The beef tastes like construction paper and the shrimp tastes like an unwiped asshole—excuse me, but it does.

17. She literally has like 20 boxes of Teddy Grahams. Fucking baby. Fucking fat baby.

18. A bitch named Janice.

19. I know they say only children are spoiled because they never had to share, but I don't think that's necessarily true. I think you could say

cont.

learn how to share." So I was like, "Fuck you, Janice," and now we don't talk. Power-hungry twat.

Okay, I'm sorry for all of my cursing and bad language, but I remember how you used to tell me to keep a diary to get out my feelings instead of yelling at my mom. And that worked for a bit but then I got lazy so I started yelling at her again. And I guess this letter is like a diary, except that it's not private because I really needed to tell someone who would actually understand me.[20]

And I know that, on the surface, this seems like not a big deal or just about soup or whatever. But it's not just about soup, you know? Because if it was just soup, I'd probably be like, "Whatever, I'll get another soup." But I'm not. I'm enraged. In a real way. And it's part of a bigger problem, which is that I feel like my life is utter shit right now and I don't see a way out of it and I feel like it's only getting worse and that thought—the thought that's it's getting worse—is even more terrifying than if I was in some kind of war zone or something where at least I would know that the war would eventually end.

Okay, I don't want to be like a total downer[21] in this whole letter. So I want to finish by telling you that you had a really good impact on my life, Miss Rita. I don't know if you re-

---

the same thing about kids who had a *lot* of siblings, because maybe they *had* to be selfish just to get anything since they were always competing. So maybe *they* don't know how to share.

20. Sorry that had to be you. ;)

21. Too late for that, right?

member but you once said something to me that meant a lot and you probably don't remember because you probably did things like that all the time for lots of girls, but for me it was the only nice thing in a year full of misery.

It was this:

One day, in the Junior Year From Hell, I was at your office and basically just crying to you.[22] And you put your hand on the top of my head in a kind of weird way[23] and you said, "You deserve to be happy."

And my mind kind of like exploded a bit. Because I realized that you were right! And that I *did* deserve to be happy, but not like in a selfish way (like I should have *more* happiness than someone else), but just in a way that's like "I'm a human being and it's okay for me to be a happy one."

And then the weirdest thing happened. About two weeks later, I got really depressed again and I decided that the only thing that would make me feel better is if someone told me "You deserve to be happy" again. But the weird rule that I made up for myself was that I couldn't *ask* anyone to tell me. It just had to *happen.*

So I would try to *lead* people into saying "You deserve to be happy" by asking weird questions to teachers and to my parents like, "What do you think we all *deserve*, like as a species?" But no one ever said the words "you deserve to be happy" and most people looked at me like I was a crazy person, which maybe I was.

---

22. As usual.
23. But in a way that I loved.

But I always pictured you saying that to me again, Miss Rita, and wished I could take a time machine back to when you first said it so I can feel your gentle hand on top of my head and hear you say it again:

"You Deserve To Be Happy."

Anyway! I should probably go, The Slutnick just walked in and I have to protect my food.[24]

Okay, I know this letter is weird and totally out of the blue but, Miss Rita, I always think about you when I'm sad.[25]

And I think you might be my only friend.

Sincerely,[26]

Harper Jablonski

P.S. The Slutnick just said, "Mind if I ask what you're writing?" And I was like, "Just a paper for class."[27]

---

24. Just kidding. Kind of.

25. Not in a bad way, not like "it makes me sad to think about you!" but "it makes me *less* sad when I do."

26. I was actually going to write "Love" but that would be weird. It's like, "too soon!"

27. Stupid bitch. Okay. Bye for real, Miss rita!

September 29

Dear Miss Rita,

Thank you so much for your letter! I am so relieved you wrote back, mainly because right after I wrote to you, I got so embarrassed. I thought you might not remember me or maybe you would hate me. But you *do* remember me and you obviously *don't* hate me.

And your letter was SO nice, even though it was kind of short.[1]

Anyway, I took your advice about being nicer to my roommate,[2] but it didn't exactly work out like I/you hoped.

Okay, so you told me that instead of secretly "harboring hatred" for The Slutnick, I should try to "engage" with her[3] and ask her if she wants to hang out.

So I did that. As soon as I finished reading your letter,[4] I asked The Slutnick if she wanted to do something outside the dorm room, like something social.

So Slutnick says, "Sure, what did you have in mind?"

---

1. And I know you told me that I should see a guidance counselor on campus, but don't worry, I wouldn't do that to you. I guess you're stuck with me forever!
2. Who you call "your roommate, Rebecca," but who I will heretofore continue to refer to as The Slutnick. Haha.
3. Which sounds a little dykey, but I know what you mean.
4. Which I read four times in a row all the way through. Obsessed much?

And I say, "Anything you want."

And I thought she would suggest something normal, like getting a cup of coffee or going to Chipotle.

But the SN says, "My sorority is holding a fundraiser tonight to raise money for Huntington's disease. Why don't you come with me and help out?"

And before I could say no to the Single Worst Invitation I've Ever Received, I said, "Sure, I'd love to."

Okay, rewind for a second!

So The Slutnick is in a sorority, which is just some bullshit way for her to make friends with other fat girls, because if she wasn't in the sorority, she would just be a fat girl with no friends.[5]

BUT. I was trying to keep an open mind like you told me to do. But not only did I have to *go* to this dumb thing, I actually had to *work* at it.

But I just kept thinking, "What would Miss Rita do?"[6]

And I thought you would probably tell me to go to the fundraiser and put a smile on my face, even if it means I'm not smiling on the inside.

And you know how hard it is for me to meet new people. I always do that thing, remember? Where I think everyone is secretly laughing at me all the time. And I was worried that I would go to the sorority thing and everyone would think I was

---

5. And bacne.
6. Like how I equate you to Jesus??

a loser because I wasn't in one[7] and I would be so embarrassed and I'd be trying to smile but actually just wanting to die.

So: The Fundraiser:

It was held at an underage music venue called the Rotting Tree[8] and the sorority was charging ten dollars admission to see some crappy local girl band named 77 Cents play their crappy feminist bullshit songs.

When we got there, it was already pretty busy.[9] And as soon as we walked in, The Slutnick immediately became a different person.[10] She started hugging everyone and squealing like an idiot and calling the other girls her "sisters" in a really forced way.[11] And she was kind of trying to include me by saying, "This is Harper, she wanted to volunteer. Isn't that SO nice?"

And the other girls were giving me hugs[12] and squealing at me and I was trying to smile, I really was, but I felt like I wanted to cry because the more hugs I got the more I felt really alone. Because the hugs felt empty or bony or not warm or something. It wasn't like when you hugged me in school, where I felt like you were not just hugging me but taking all the pain away with your hug. Like you were hugging the sad-

---

7. Because they're fucking dumb.
8. Makes sense that the trees in St. Louis are rotting.
9. Not surprising since this town is made up of total losers with nothing to do.
10. Although still just as fat.
11. Yup. Twenty white girls calling each other "sister" like they're singing backup at the Cotton Club.
12. I probably contracted bacne.

ness *out* of my body.[13] I wish I could be back in New York and get a hug from you again! Just one more hug from Miss Rita![14] *Anyway!*

The sorority was also holding a raffle, which is apparently where I came in. I was supposed to work with some "sister" named Stephanie selling raffle tickets to the unfortunate losers who showed up to see 77 Cents. So The Slutnick introduces me to Stephanie and I was like, "Whoa!" because she had like a *humongously* bony nose.[15]

And then The Slutnick runs off to meet the band. So I was *stuck* with this bony-nosed freak who I didn't even know and I started to feel that panicky feeling again, where my heart starts racing and my breathing becomes weird. And Bony Nose probably sees that I'm panicking so she says to me, "Don't worry, I'm a really nice boss."[16]

But instead, I just said, "Thanks, Steph."

And then Stephanie told me what my degrading job would be. I had to walk around like an idiot selling people raffle tickets. It was three dollars for one ticket, five for two, or twenty dollars for a string of tickets as long as the person's arm.[17]

---

13. Just tell me if I get too weird. Sorry.
14. Okay, now *I* sound dykey.
15. So I knew she'd be mean (because she was dealt a bad hand—or bad *nose!* hehe—in life).
16. And I was thinking, "You're not my boss at all. You're just another ugly outcast who's part of some dumb sorority cause she's too ugly to make friends on her own."
17. Which was the most embarrassing part of all because I had to

cont.

I felt so strange. I didn't know *anyone* there and now I have to walk around and be nice and try to sell them shit?

And then to make matters worse, Stephanie asked, "Do you want to meet Jocelyn?"

So I was like, "Who's Jocelyn?"

And Stephanie's like, "Taryn's older sister. She has Huntington's. She's the reason we're all here."

And before I could say no to the *Second* Worst Invitation I've Ever Received, I said, "Sure, I'd love to."

And then this weird woman started limping toward us.[18]

And Stephanie waves her over and says, "Jocelyn, I want you to meet Harper. She's Becca's roommate and was kind enough to volunteer her time tonight."

And then Jocelyn stuttered, "Thanks for v-v-volunteering."[19]

But I didn't say anything because I didn't know if I was supposed to respond to her or just wait for her to go away.

And then she reached out to shake my hand, but her hand was like quivering.[20] It freaked me out, so I just kind of waved at her. And I could tell she felt bad that I didn't want to shake

---

measure the tickets against their arms to see how many they should get and it was also sexist because men have longer arms so they got more tickets. I brought this fact up to my "boss" and she was confused because she's an idiot and my "issue" was obviously too smart for her.

18. You guessed it. Fucking Jocelyn.

19. And a little spit came out with her *V*'s, which I tried to duck and avoid.

20. It actually looked like when someone is turning into a werewolf and their bones are crackling and moving inside their skin.

her hand, but it was like, "Stop trembling uncontrollably and *then* maybe I'll touch you."[21]

When Jocelyn finally walked away, Stephanie turned to me and said, "You were really rude to her. She's probably gonna die soon and you were just really rude."

And then Stephanie walked away and left me there alone with my roll of raffle tickets.

That's when I started crying. At that moment, I became homesick for everything, not just my home, but everything in the past. I wished I was back at literally *any* other time in my past. Even the single worst day of my life[22] was better than this one.

I ran backstage, looking for Slutnick because she was the only familiar thing in the whole place. But I couldn't find her anywhere. And the band was gearing up to go on stage.

I ran around the Rotting Tree looking for Slutnick, but I couldn't find her anywhere. So I ran to the bathroom, still crying, because I thought I had to puke. And I put my head over the toilet and gagged, but all that came out was a little thick white spit.

And with my forehead resting on the bowl, I heard the band start to play their shitty song, which was loud and fast and angry and the main girl just kept screaming, "I'm stuck inside, under your glass ceiling, stuck inside and I can't break out!"

---

21. Okay, maybe that sounds evil, but seriously, I don't know if she's contagious, right?
22. Jenny Seifert's Sweet Sixteen, remember?

And I was breathing fast and my heart was racing in time with their shitty song, as I tried to puke.

Then I ran outside for some fresh air[23] and something took over inside me and I just decided to run home. I was still holding the big roll of raffle tickets but I just ran and ran and ran till I made it home.

And I was so miserable, I really couldn't take it anymore, so I decided to do something that I'd been thinking about doing for months.[24]

I should probably backtrack and tell you something else, which is that, over the summer, I was prescribed antidepressants, but I didn't start taking them because I was too scared. I didn't know what it would do to me or if I'd suddenly get totally fat or something. And it had a weird name, it was called Lexapro,[25] so I never took them. But, just in case, I packed the bottle at the bottom of my suitcase and took it up to school with me.

But since I was so unbelievably upset, I decided that even getting fat wasn't worth feeling this shitty.

So I dug through my suitcase and found the bottle. And I took one of the little white pills out and stuffed it in the back of my mouth. And since I was crying so much, I still had a lot

---

23. Which is an oxymoron in St. Louis.
24. Don't worry, I didn't try to kill myself!
25. Which, if you ask me, sounds like some kind of evil dinosaur, Tyrannosaurus Lexapro.

of tears and mucus in my mouth,[26] so I was able to swallow the pill without water.

Then I took a deep breath, waiting to feel better, and curled up in my bed, over my covers, still in my clothes. And I tried to go to sleep, but the weirdest thing happened. I got really dizzy and I started shivering in bed. Like shaking. Uncontrollably.

And I immediately regretted taking the Lexapro and vowed to never take anything like that again because I'm really sensitive to medications and it was making me feel so weirded out.

And I thought I might actually die. Like I thought, "Oh. This is what it feels like before you die."

And I felt so crazy, I was shaking on the bed like I was freezing even though I was sweating through my clothes. And my whole body was shivering and I started to wonder if this is what it was like to have Huntington's disease—to always feel like your body is not yours to control. And if this is how Jocelyn felt all the time. And then I kind of wished I *had* shaken her hand because I really wanted someone to touch me right now.

And I never thought I'd actually say this, but I started wishing Slutnick would come home.[27]

And I don't know how much time passed, but it felt like hours before I heard the door open and the distinct sound of

---

26. I know that's gross, but I'm trying to be honest.
27. Don't use that against me!

Slutnick's thighs scraping together as she came in through the door.

The light was so harsh on my face, but I have never been more relieved. Slutnick said, "Harper?"

And I said, "Yeah?"

And she was like, "I was SO worried about you."

And I said, "You were?" kind of surprised.

And she said, "We all were. You just ran out. Are you okay?"[28]

And I was shaking so hard that I did something I still can't believe. I said, "Can you come hold me?"

And Slutnick didn't say anything. She just walked to my bed, laid down, and put her arms around me.

I think she could see that I was crying so she said, "It's gonna be okay."

And I was *this* close to calling her Slutnick, but I stopped myself just in time to say, "Thanks, Becca."

And she said, "It's okay."

And I asked, "Why are you being so nice to me?"

And Slutnick said, "We're sisters."

And even though I thought it was weird to call me a "sister" because a) I'm not in the sorority with her, and b) we're not two black women in a Harlem church choir, I started

---

28. I thought she'd be pissed that I ran out with the raffle tickets. Or that I didn't tell Stephanie that I was leaving the Rotting Tree. Or that I was rude to Jocelyn, who was going to die soon. But she wasn't. She was just *worried* about me. Weird.

crying again. Because, for the first time since I got to this shit-hole of a school, I didn't feel totally homesick.

And I nuzzled my nose into Slutnick's rolls of stomach fat and thought, "There's nowhere else I'd rather be."

And Slutnick hugged me tighter—a real, emotional hug. A hug that made me want to stay in her arms forever and totally change my life to be exactly like her. Because even though she's a fat fucking frizzy-haired bitch,[29] sometimes you just need to be hugged.

I bet you thought I would end this letter with something bitchy or mean[30] but I actually feel kind of okay for the moment.

I hope you do too, Miss Rita.

Love,[31]

Harper Jablonski

---

29. With bad breath and acne all over her flabby back.
30. And there's still time . . .
31. I hope it's okay to write "Love"! I'm not a dyke, Miss Rita! I just feel a lot of things.

October 5

Dear Miss Rita,

Well, it finally happened. Yesterday, I fell in love!

It started out like a fairy tale!

Unfortunately, it did not end like one.[1]

I loved and lost, Miss Rita. And I know they say "It's better to have loved and lost than never to have loved at all," but, after yesterday, I think I disagree with them.[2]

Here is what happened:

Okay, so yesterday I was in a macroeconomics class. It's a morning class and I'm usually really tired during it so I'm not always paying full attention. Also, it's a lecture class, which is super boring and taught by this tiny Indian woman with a full Indian accent[3] who has ZERO sense of humor.

So we were talking about something that didn't make any sense, which was having to choose between guns and butter in an economy.[4] So she asked us, if we were running the country, what would *we* choose and why. So I raised my hand and said, "I would choose guns because, if you have guns, you can invade the people who have the butter and take it from them."

---

1. Unless that fairy tale is "Little Red Riding Hood," because essentially I was eaten by a wolf.
2. I know it's wrong to disagree with a major quotation, but, Miss Rita, listen to what happened to me and then decide.
3. As if macroeconomics wasn't already hard enough to understand.
4. Sorry if I'm putting you to sleep already, Miss R.

And the professor woman kind of smiled, like I was making a joke or something,[5] and then said, "Anybody else?"

And then this kid who's usually pretty quiet raised his hand and the Indian woman said, "Yes, Ryan?"

And he goes, "I think Harper makes a good point actually. If you have weapons, it gives you control over resources, even if it means taking them by force."

And then the Indian woman smiled at Ryan and said, "Harper and Ryan make a good team, class. Their point is not without historical precedence actually."

And then she continued talking about guns and butter so I do what I normally do, which is tune her out and think about literally anything else.[6]

And something really strange happened to me, Miss Rita. I started dreaming about this boy. This Ryan boy.

I thought, "Maybe we *are* a good team." I've never actually *looked* at him before, but now that we were a *team*, I really started to notice how great he is.[7]

---

5. Which I wasn't. And which I still think is a good idea.

6. Sorry if this sounds irresponsible but I'm taking this class pass/fail cause I knew I wouldn't do well in it.

7. Okay, it's important for me to tell you that I *still* have not had a boyfriend, Miss Rita. You probably remember that, in junior year, I was a virgin? Well, guess what? Still a card-carrying member. ;) I don't know why, I'm sure I could have lost it a million times but I just never did. I actually never even really kissed a boy except one time, in seventh grade, when this asshole Russian kid named Alexey chased me around the school parking lot and kissed me on the head. But that felt

cont.

And then my mind just started to go crazy, Miss Rita. The class was two hours and I think I totally spaced for the whole rest of the class, just dreaming about my *teammate* Ryan.

And my vagina started like tingling! I was like, "*Whoa* down there! Didn't realize you did *that*!" I thought I would maybe start peeing, but it felt so good, like electricity running through my body from my vag to my heart!

I just couldn't stop staring at Ryan, who turned into this like beautiful perfect creature to me!

And, Miss Rita, sitting there in class, I worked out our whole lives together![8]

First Date:

It would be romantic but would NOT end with too much physical activity.[9] I would be coquettish[10] and we would go to an Italian restaurant like Romano's Macaroni Grill[11] and I would order something sensible like salmon, which is easy to eat on a date because it doesn't have any sauce and it's not pasta, which you CANNOT eat on a date because it's impossible and makes your mouth look stupid and has sauce. Ryan

---

more like an attack than a kiss. :(And then he said something in Russian, which is an ugly-sounding language, and then he laughed a little, which also sounded ugly.

8. Please don't think I'm totally crazy.

9. I'm not a prude, Miss Rita, but guys get grossed out when you do too much on the first date.

10. Which means flirty but not slutty.

11. There are two in St. Louis. One is a shithole and the other one's decent. We would go to the decent one. Obviously.

would probably get the steak cause he's such a guy. And then he would drive me home and, before I got out of the car, he would put his hand on the back of my neck and it would feel so nice and I would know what was coming next.

And he would lean in[12] and I would let him kiss me once on the lips. A light, crisp kiss. And he would say, "I had a great time, Harper," and I would just smile. I wouldn't say anything! I wouldn't say "I did too." I would just smile and maybe bite my bottom lip *coquettishly* to keep him wondering, "Did she have a good time? Does she like me? *Who is she??*"

Second Date:

Ryan would invite me to hang out with his friends at his house.[13] It will be a Sunday afternoon. And I would sit on the couch while the guys played video games and drank Pabst.[14] And at some point, Ry-Ry would sneak his sweet little hand into mine. And we'd interlace our fingers, and when one of the roommates made a dumb joke, Ryan would look at me and secretly roll his eyes and I'd secretly roll my eyes too. And then he'd ask if I wanted to go for a little walk and we would walk outside, still holding hands and feeling so special because the friends would still be playing video games and they'd be thinking that me and Ryan were so cool because we had a secret relationship where we sneak out for walks

---

12. I would stay totally still though, so I don't look like a ho-bag.
13. He probably lives off campus in a dingy house with a few other guys.
14. They're SO typical. But it's cute, you know?

together. Then Ryan would say something like, "I really like you." And *this* time, I *would* answer him back. I would say, "I like you too, Ryan."[15]

And then, after we took the walk, we would head back into the house and walk right past his friends and go upstairs to his bedroom. My heart would be racing so fast because I'd know what would be coming. He would hold my waist and lean in and kiss me. And then we would fall onto the bed and we would be making out. And it would be SO nice. And then I would let him grab my breast[16] but OVER my clothes. And then he would try to put his hand UNDER my shirt and I would say, "Maybe next time, mister."[17]

Third Date:

The third date wouldn't even be a date, Miss Rita. It would just be a farewell party. To my virginity!!! Sayonara Sucker! I would let Ryan have it. Own it. It would be his. The way it would work is that Ryan would text me late one night:

RYAN: What r u doin?
ME: Nothin. Just chillin.
RYAN: Wanna come over?
ME: Sure.

---

15. I wouldn't say "I *really* like you" though. Because I still need to hold on to some of my mystique. Otherwise, I'm just another two-bit slut, which Ryan could find anywhere.
16. Guys are obsessed with grabbing breasts apparently.
17. How great is that???

It would be SO romantic, Miss Rita. I would sneak out of the dorm, past Slutnick, past the clueless night guards, and run to Ryan's house. As I approach, I would notice a single light on in the upstairs bedroom, where Ryan would be waiting, having already showered.

I would throw a pebble at his window. He would come down and without talking[18] we would hold hands as we walked up to his bedroom. And there, we would start making out on his bed. And he would immediately put his hand up my shirt[19] and he would kiss every part of me, Miss Rita!

And while Ryan was lying on top of me, he would breathlessly ask, "Is it okay if I enter you Harper?" And I would say, also breathlessly, "Access granted, Ryan."

And then he would fuck me, in and out of me, so nicely for hours until I bled all over his bed, but he wouldn't care and we would do laundry together the next day and scrub out my hymen together.

And after a few weeks of Ryan and I dating and spending every day together, I would tell him that I haven't gotten my period in a while and I'm wondering if everything is okay. And Ryan would just take my hand and say, "Harper, I did this on purpose. I want to start a family with you!"

And then we would move in together. I would ditch Slutnick and Ryan would ditch his dumb roommates and we would find a nice place off campus to raise our children. And

---

18. Nothing else needs to be said.
19. And I would LET him this time. A promise is a promise.

after we graduate, I would stay home with the kids and Ryan would work his way up the corporate ladder.[20]

Oh, Miss Rita, it would be wonderful! My life would be complete!

If only it were true. What really happened was this:

After class, I walked up to him[21] and said,

ME: Hey, Ryan.

RYAN: (looking like he might not know who I am) Hey . . .
(clearly can't remember my name)

ME: Harper . . .

RYAN: Right. Harper.

ME: Are you doing anything after class?

RYAN: You mean now?

ME: Well, yeah, I guess. (I laugh *coquettishly*) I guess that is now.

---

20. I know what you're thinking—this is not 1950, Harper. But, Miss Rita, I'm a traditionalist. I want a traditional life with Ryan. I don't care that it's not empowering or whatever. I want a regular, run-of-the-mill American thing with him. Yes, I want the white picket fence! Yes, I want the 2.5 kids! And yes, I want the SUV and the washer/dryer and gravy on my Thanksgiving turkey! I don't care if that makes me old-fashioned. I want our children to *know* their mother, I want Ryan to feel complete and accomplished in the workplace. Sorry, Gloria Steinman. Sorry. :(

21. In my mind, we were already married, so I probably looked really weird to him. Like *my face* probably looked like a housewife, running out to meet her longtime husband, and *his face* probably looked like a kid coming out of an economics class being approached by a crazed stranger.

RYAN: I gotta pick my girlfriend up from work. Why?

ME: Oh, nothing. Have a good day. Bye. (walks away)

END OF SCENE.[22]

Oh, Miss RIIIIITTTTTTAAAAAA! I felt like such a fool! What was I thinking? I was so embarrassed. I don't know what was going through my mind. He didn't even remember my name, Miss Rita! I was nothing to him. Nothing. And he had a girlfriend!

I was at the lowest moment of my entire life, Miss Rita. I just wished I was dead. Like literally dead though. Like inside-a-coffin-rotting-away-from-a-disease dead.

And just as I thought I would have to go home and kill myself, something washed over me. A weird, new feeling.

As Ryan walked away, I started to realize that I didn't want to be with him anyway.[23]

I started noticing all this other stuff about him that made me so relieved to not be with him anymore. First of all, he dresses like a fucking hobo teenager—his pants were loose and sagging around his waist.[24] And his hairline was actually receding[25] so he put gel in his hair and slicked it forward. Who are you kidding, Ryan? You're going to be a bald fuckface who will probably also get really fat because once you're bald you're

---

22. And End of Life! Just like that, my life ended. Everything. My butter turned into a gun!
23. And that I dodged a *major* bullet.
24. I guess he bought them from a time machine store!
25. Hahahahaha!!! He's gonna be so bald!

already too ugly to get fucked so you may as well fuck food for a living and get really fucking chubs.

I can't believe I almost threw it all away for *that*. My precious virginity for that fat douchebag bald garbage can man.

And his girlfriend *"works"*? How old is she? She's probably like sixty years old, like a fucking granny, in huge panties who's fucked so many guys in her long life as an old hippie with white person dreadlocks and armpit hair. And Ryan probably has STDs all over his stupid dick. And I should probably warn his girlfriend, but she probably already knows because *she's* the whore who gave him the STDs in the first place. "Gotta pick my girlfriend up from work." Probably means he's going to a brothel.[26]

Once I realized how shitty Ryan was as a life partner, I felt SO much better. My whole body relaxed and I actually thought I was so lucky to have gone through our whole life together because it made me realize how AWFUL it would actually be to share it with "Ryan."

Because the truth is, Miss Rita, some people are destined to be alone forever because they're too disgusting for anyone to actually fall in love with them, but I am destined to be alone forever because I'm too unique and independent minded.[27]

---

26. Because his girlfriend is most likely a whore.

27. And I don't need a *man* to complete me. Sorry, boys. But I am fine on my own. I know who I am and what I need and I'm sorry if that scares people away. My fierce independence. My strong willpower. I'm going to be a strong single female like Eleanor Roosevelt or Janis Joplin. I will live alone, not like a dyke with a buzz cut and bad breath, but

cont.

Miss Rita, I guess this is what they call growth.[28] I finally realize who I am.

I am a woman.

Hear me roar.[29]

In solidarity,

Harper Jablonski[30]

---

like a beautiful woman who owns her body. I don't need a man to tell me what I can and can't do. Especially a fucking old-fashioned, stuck-in-a-time-warp brute like *Ryan*.

28. The good kind. Not the fat kind.

29. Not literally. That'd be gross. ;)

30. You can bet I will never change my name! Not even hyphenating it. I will make no phallic compromises!

October 18

Dear Miss Rita,

Sometimes, things seem fucking awful, but if you look at them a different way, they're actually not.[1]

I had a really weird night this week that made me think a lot about my life and my parents and what I want to be when I get older.[2]

Okay, here's what happened:

Slutnick and I don't have class on Wednesday[3] so we were just hanging out in our room[4] and Slutnick was showing me the grossest video of a snake eating a whole crocodile. It was so disgusting, but I couldn't stop watching it.

And just before the end of the video, there was a knock on the door. It was kind of a silly knock, like the one where you knock a few times in a funny beat and wait for the other person to finish the beat.

And SN opened the door and two old fugly people were standing there, grinning like idiots. And Slutnick squealed, "Oh my god, what are you guys doing here?"

---

1. You know?
2. Which is actually coming pretty soon, if you think about it. You probably didn't think you would be old when you were my age, right?
3. Actually, Slutnick never has class (get it? Cause she's a slut).
4. I should also mention here that SN's been pretty tolerable recently. We're actually getting along and she's not being such a massive douchebag.

And the old fuglies said, "We wanted to surprise you and take you to dinner!"

And then all three fat, ugly people were holding hands and jumping up and down.

That's when I realized I was looking at Mr. and Mrs. Slutnick.

The dad looked like Chef Boyardee but if he was uglier and more Jewy and not wearing a chef's hat. And the mom looked like Slutnick if she kept getting fatter and uglier and just went through life without ever making any of the right moves.

Slutnick introduced me, saying, "This is my friend Harper."[5]

I shook The Slutnicks' hands and the dad smiled real wide and said, "If it isn't the famous Harper!" and the mom said, "We've heard so many things about you!"

And I just said, "Okay," because I didn't know what she meant because she didn't say "I've heard so many *good* things" or "*bad* things." Just "things."

Then Slutnick asked if I could come with them to dinner and the dad said, "Of course!" And then in a silly vampire voice, "We've come for both of you! Mwahaha!"

And Slutnick squealed again and hugged the elder Slutnicks, saying, "This is so exciting!"

---

5. Okay, I know this seems like not a big deal, but she said *friend* not *roommate*, which actually made me feel SO good, Miss Rita, because a "friend" is someone you *choose* to know and a "roommate" is someone you're *forced* to know.

When we got in the SNs' car, the dad said, "Jill and I were thinking Olive Garden, does that sound good?"

And Slutnick shouted, "Yay!"[6] and did a little dance.

As we drove to the restaurant, the three SNs all talked at the same time, so excited, like they hadn't seen each other in years. And I wanted to hate them so much but, more than anything, it just made me miss being with my family and it made me pissed that my parents would never think to surprise me.[7] They asked Slutnick about school and knew all of her professors' names and knew exactly how she was doing in her classes. It was so bizarre. My parents didn't even ask me what classes I was *taking*.

At the Olive Garden, we had to wait for a table and they gave us a little vibrating stick[8] to let us know when our table was ready.

And while we were waiting, the SNs made a big deal about how happy they were to be eating there, saying things like, "I can't wait to dive into their Bolognese," and "I think we should get a flatbread. You know, *for the table*."[9]

---

6. As though they asked her if she would like a winning lottery ticket. Although, I guess, to The Slutnick, food is like winning the lottery.
7. Okay, so my parents live much farther away from school, but they would never think to surprise me even if school was right around the *corner*. My parents never did anything fun or spontaneous or interesting without making a big show of how great they were for doing it, you know?
8. The closest thing Slutnick would ever get to a date.
9. Sure, blame the table for eating all the food.

And Slutnick said, "You guys know what my favorite part of dinner is, don't you?"

And the parents said, at the same time, "Unlimited breadsticks!"

And SN squealed with piggish delight.[10]

Then they asked me what I wanted and I didn't know what to say because I didn't know the whole menu like they did, so I just said, "Oh, I think I don't like Italian food." I don't know why I said that, Miss Rita, I really do like Italian food. I just got nervous, so I blurted that out.

Then the parents looked kind of disappointed in me and asked, "Do you want to go somewhere else, Harper?" And I *should've* said, "No, this is great. I actually love Italian food," but instead I said, "Okay."

Luckily, the vibrating thing buzzed and our table was ready, so the dad said, "Well, let's do Olive Garden for now and we'll let you choose the restaurant next time." And I thought this was actually really nice because it meant that they wanted me to go with them *next* time even if I screwed up tonight.[11]

Miss Rita, I have to say, eating with The Slutnicks was actually kind of great. They're really funny people and they tried

---

10. And I was thinking that the combination of The Slutnicks and unlimited breadsticks would put the Olive Garden out of business.
11. In the lobby of the Olive Garden, there was a sign that said, WHEN YOU'RE HERE, YOU'RE FAMILY. And I thought, since I'm here, I'm part of their family. And that made me feel good even though I didn't want to be part of their family because it would mean I would probably have to get fatter and uglier.

to include me in the conversation the whole time. The dad talked about his bicycling trip to the Amish country, where he stayed in a real Amish person's house overnight, and the mom talked about her book club, and it was funny how she described it as kind of juvenile, saying it reminded her of being in a high school English class with overly emotional teenagers arguing with each other.

My parents barely speak to each other and never do anything fun. My dad comes home really late every night, and if my mom or I ask him about his day, he says, "Can we please not talk about that right now?" And my mother has no friends that she actually likes and would never join a book club because that would require reading, which she refuses to do.

But The Slutnicks seemed like they were *actually* happy people and it was really weird to see that. My parents always *pretend* to be happy when they're with strangers but it's so clear that they're pretending. But The Slutnicks seemed happy with their lives and with each other. And I guess I never realized that was possible.[12]

And they asked me about myself, if I liked school, which I said no to, and then told me that "the first year is always the hardest and don't worry too much about enjoying it." It was

---

12. But even though they were nice, it was a little disgusting watching them eat. I don't know if you've ever been to a farm, Miss Rita, where you can watch pigs eat from a trough and then roll around in their own shit, but that's what it looked like watching The Slutnicks go at their spaghetti Bolognese.

strange advice to give, but it made me feel more relaxed about school.[13]

Miss Rita, it was such a nice dinner, I felt like I was a real Slutnick. We got dessert[14] and coffee and The Slutnicks paid for dinner and then thanked *us* for coming with *them*: "It was so great of you girls to come out with us tonight. What a treat."

On the way home, Miss Rita, I'm not kidding, I talked the whole way! I couldn't believe it. I usually never talk around other people because I'm so freaked out that I'll say something stupid or something I don't know about and then they'll ask me about it and I won't know what to say. But I just couldn't help myself, I told the SNs everything about me, even stuff I never thought about before, like what I want to do for a profession.[15] I even told them about you, Miss Rita.[16]

And then they dropped us off at the dorm and gave us both a hug and then the dad said to me, "I'm glad you're taking care of my daughter." I couldn't believe it. *I* was taking care of *her.* I don't even know if they were being serious, but it made me feel so good. I've never taken care of anyone and suddenly

---

13. When I told my mother that I hated school, she said, "For what we're paying to send you there, you better start liking it." And I was like, "Fuck off, Mom."

14. Tiramisu and cannolis *for the table.*

15. To which I said, "Fashion," cause I never thought about it before and I got nervous and I thought that sounded good.

16. But I just said I have a "mentor" from high school. And they said, "She sounds really supportive." Not bad, huh?

I was taking care of Slutnick! It made me feel like an adult. Like I was important. And *needed*.

Slutnick and I went back up to our room and I was still smiling so so wide. I wanted to take a shower to wash the Olive Garden smell out of my hair[17] but I thought it would be nice to ask Slutnick if she wanted to shower first. So I did. And she said, "Sure, thanks for asking, Harp!"[18]

Slutnick took her towel and soap and toothbrush and left the room to shower and I walked around the dorm room, alone.

I looked at all of our shared possessions. Our coffeemaker. Our microwave. Our minifridge with the permanent coffee stain running down the middle. Our toaster. Our crusty garbage can. Our dollar store plates and aluminum forks. Our whiteboard with the scrawled neon green note, "Coffeemaker's busted."

Then I looked at Slutnick's possessions. Her hair straightener. Her eyelash curler. Her half-eaten jar of Nutella. Her ticket stubs from every concert she's ever been to. Her corkboard with pictures of fugly friends from home.

And then I looked at my possessions. My anthro books for school. My laptop with a sticker of a bloody apple covering the regular apple logo. My faded security blanket from home. My XXL shirt from Floor Wars. My bulk foods from Costco.

---

17. Fettuccini Alfredo mixed with budget marinara.
18. She actually called me Harp. I never had a nickname before, and if you'd asked me a week ago if I wanted one, I would have thought it was so stupid, but I actually *liked* Harp.

And I thought that maybe I would like it if Slutnick used my stuff more. Like maybe I would be happier sharing stuff with her than just keeping it to myself. Like maybe it would make me happier to know she was eating my ramen than if I were actually eating it myself.[19]

And then I started thinking about my own parents. And I really tried to think about them in a *neutral* way. You know? Like I tried to think about them as though I wasn't their daughter for a minute. Just think about them as though I was a person looking at the situation. And I got really mad at them.

They knew how lonely I was up here and they never did anything to make me feel better or *needed*. When I asked them if they were going to visit me during the semester, my mother said that they thought I needed to "cultivate my own experiences for the first few months."[20] And after one night with The Slutnicks, I already felt more loved and part of a family than I did in eighteen years with my own parents.

Slutnick came back in with a towel wrapped around her head like a Muslim man.[21] And her whole body was red and blotchy from the hot water. And I immediately felt a little embarrassed because she looked kind of fat and I thought it was embarrassing that I had a fat roommate and I was worried

---

19. I know that sounds weird or like illogical, like, "How would someone *else* eating ramen make *me* happy?" But I actually did feel like it would make me happy to know that Slutnick was happy. Strange.
20. Which meant no.
21. Is that racist? I'm not sure. She really did look like that.

people would think *I* was fat, just by association. And then I tried to remember that thinking that way was mean and also probably not exactly right.

Then Slutnick said, "Should we finish watching the snake video?"

And I snapped out of my thinking about her being fat and got so excited. I had totally forgotten about the video.

Slutnick opened her computer, which was paused two-thirds into the video, and pressed play:

It was so gross, Miss Rita. The snake ate the entire crocodile and then slithered around with it inside of him.[22] And I wanted to hate the snake for eating the crocodile, but then I thought, "Maybe it's none of my business."

And I looked at Slutnick and she was grossed out too. And I laughed to myself because I pictured us from the snake's point of view: two girls, making the same grossed-out face, staring at me as I slithered around with a crocodile inside of my body.

And I realized that, to the snake, Slutnick and I were probably not that different.

And then I thought that the snake probably thought we were related to each other. And maybe he's right, maybe Slutnick and I *are* related.

And maybe that's what life is about—finding families in different places. Like maybe, this year, Slutnick and I are a

---

22. It was so weird, you could see the outline of the crocodile inside the snake's body!

family. And maybe next year, I'll have a different roommate and *she'll* be my family.

And in a way, this thought made me feel really alone and also really *not* alone at the same time.

Because it meant that *everyone* could be my family but *no one* was permanent.

Well, except for you, Miss Rita.

Thanks!

Love,

Harp[23]

---

23. Only you and SN have permission to call me that. ;)

November 7

Dear Miss Rita,

I wasn't going to write to you because I thought I'd leave you alone, but something absolutely horrifying happened to me and I don't know whether I should go to the police or buy a gun or what. So far, I haven't told anyone about it,[1] but keeping it inside is no longer a possibility.

I think I may have been sexually assaulted by a teacher.[2]

I'll start at the beginning so you know how this developed.

I'm taking an Intro to Anthro class, which is basically about different cultures around the world and why they're weird.[3] My professor is a young guy who so desperately wants to be like the "cool" professor. He dresses in "cool" flannel shirts and "cool" jeans and has long hair down to his shoulders. I guess he's maybe a tiny bit attractive but it's so fucking annoying how all the girls in class basically orgasm when he calls on them.[4]

---

1. Except you. And please keep it a secret till we figure out what to do.

2. I don't mean to scare you, but it's true. Yup. Welcome to college, Harper.

3. A word I've been told is not appropriate.

4. I even overheard this one whore, Sarah Stein, say, "I want to fuck him so bad." And he's *always* calling on Sarah. It's so irritating.

His name is Mr. Garrett, but let's call him Mr. Doe for the purposes of this letter, in case there's a court case or a lawsuit or whatever.

The last three classes were about something called Female Genital Mutilation, which is the most disgusting thing I've ever heard about in my life.[5] It is where these evil African men cut the vaginas off poor African women. The men do it for the most disgusting, selfish reasons: because it feels better for their huge dumb penises when they stick them in the poor women's tiny, mutilated vagina holes.

Men are so fucking terrifying, Miss Rita. Everything about them is so disgusting and scary! And after my "encounter" with Mr. Doe, I just want to cut off every man's dumb stupid penis and stick it in his dumb eye socket![6]

And what's so fucked up about this whole thing is that Mr. Doe actually made us write a paper about why Female Genital Mutilation is a *good* thing.[7] We were supposed to "incorporate" what we've learned about other cultures and their specific customs to explain why cutting a woman's vagina is a *good* thing. I could not even believe it.

When he asked if we had any questions, I raised my hand and Sarah Steinwhore raised her hand. I was going to ask how we could possibly write a paper *supporting* that evil bullshit,

---

5. Have you heard of this? Look it up if you haven't but try not to anger puke.
6. I know that's totally graphic, but I have actually pictured doing this to Mr. Doe.
7. Yes, you read that correctly. We were asked to write a paper on why the Single Most Evil Thing in the World was <u>GOOD</u>.

but Mr. Doe called on Steinwhore instead of me. And the fucking kiss-ass asked, "Is there a length to the paper or can we write as much as we want?"[8]

And Mr. Doe said, "Sure, Sarah, you can go as long as you feel you need to make your point."

So I went back to my dorm to start working on this paper, which I didn't think I should write in the first place.

And Slutnick was in the room, reading *Beowulf.* And she and I are getting along really well now because she's being less of a bitch and I'm being more "open-minded."[9]

So I told SN that I have to write this paper about why cutting off an African woman's vagina is a good thing and she was horrified. And she said she was just reading about Beowulf killing Grendel's mother after she tried to revenge her son's death. Beowulf killed the *mother* of his enemy! Which is so unbelievably typical. And I realized that *all* men throughout history—Beowulf, African guys, Mr. Doe—*all men* are fucking evil pricks.

And I felt really conflicted. Because I had to write this paper for class, but I also knew that it was the wrong thing to do. So I did a little "soul search," which you taught me about in junior year.

And that's when I realized I could not write this paper.

---

8. She *should* have asked, "How long does it take to wipe your shit off of my nose after class?" Because she's a brown-nosing bitch.
9. Thanks to you, Miss Rita.

So I sat down at my computer and started writing what I thought I *should* write instead. It was this:[10]

> Throughout the various countries of Africa, a wide-spread problem is occurring. It is called Female Genital Mutilation. Female genital mutilation (FGM), also known as female genital cutting and female circumcision, is defined by the World Health Organization (WHO) as "all procedures that involve partial or total removal of the external female genitalia or other injury to the female genital organs for non-medical reasons" (Wikipedia).
>
> I was asked by my Intro to Anthro teacher, Mr. Garrett, to write a paper on why this is a good thing.
>
> But I can't.
>
> Because it's not.
>
> A good thing.
>
> FGM is a disgusting practice that men do to women because they want their vaginas to be smaller because it feels better on their penises when they have sex. If anyone thinks this is a good thing, they are disgustingly wrong.
>
> Men have controlled everything in the world for centuries now, be it banking, sports, or the automobile industry. And it's time for that to change. They think because they have penises or are taller than women, they can control them.
>
> FGM has to stop right now and the men who do it

---

10. Sorry to include my whole paper, but it's important for backstory!

should have to have *their* penises cut to see how much *they* like it. If I could, I would fly to Africa to cut off all the men's penises.[11] And I would put all the African penises in a huge blender and make all the men watch as their penises blended together in a bloody penis shake. And then I would make them drink the penis shake until they puked, then I'd probably have them eat the penis shake puke.[12]

But since I can't go to Africa because of the diseases, I will instead start here in St. Louis, cutting off the penises of all the men who abuse their wives. And all the rapists and bartenders who bother women all the time. I'll cut their penises off too.

And, actually, while I'm at it, Mr. Garrett? I'll cut your penis off too. I see how you look at some of the girls in class. You're using your power of authority to flirt, I see that. And the fact that you're asking us to write this paper is proof that you support the evil African Empire men who want to cut off women's vaginas for their own evil pleasure.

Well, guess what, men? And guess what, Mr. Garrett? Your time is up!

---

11. Okay, this is where the paper starts getting a little nuts.
12. I don't know what I was thinking, Miss Rita. I know this is totally disgusting of me. I think I just got carried away!

That was my paper. I read it to Slutnick and she thought it was amazing. She literally was like, "Harper, that's the most shocking thing I've ever heard."

So, the next morning, I put the paper in Mr. Doe's mailbox.

We didn't have anthro class till Tuesday, so I had the whole weekend and Monday to think about what Mr. Doe would think when he read it. And the more I thought about it, the more excited I got. I felt more and more confident that what I wrote was not only really smart, but actually a good thing for the world.[13]

On Tuesday, I went to class as usual but I had a nervous excitement in my belly, like when you're waiting to see who's going to get kicked off *American Idol.* And Mr. Doe came in like nothing was wrong. I was wondering if he'd even read the papers. Luckily Steinwhore raised her hand and asked, "Will we be getting our papers back today?"[14]

And Mr. Doe said, "Yes, I've read and graded them all and will return them at the end of class. By the way, very good job all of you."

I was so confused. How could he have read and graded them and not said anything about mine?

Anyway, he didn't even talk about Female Genital Mutilation once during class. Instead, he started a new lesson about

---

13. One of my favorite quotations is "Well-behaved women seldom make history." I guess I'm making some history.
14. Something tells me Steinwhore didn't write about cutting Mr. Doe's penis off.

Nanook of the North, some dumb movie about an Eskimo who lied about getting in a boat.

And when class was ending, Mr. Doe said, "Before I forget, I have your papers. Some really interesting work this week, you guys."

Then he silently handed out the papers, and when he got to me, he just casually put it on my desk as though I hadn't written an essay about cutting off his penis. I looked at the first page, there were no comments. And I flipped to the back, where there was a small note that said, "See me after class. — Mr. G."

I didn't know what to expect. I thought he might be a little mad about the Penis Shake line, but otherwise, I thought I wrote a really thoughtful essay.

After everyone left the room, I stayed at my desk.

Mr. Doe came up and sat in the desk next to mine. My heart was beating so quick. I didn't know if he was going to congratulate me or yell at me or what.

He started, "So, I read your paper, Harper."

I didn't say anything. He kept talking:

"I understand that you feel very strongly about this issue. It's clear that it raised a lot of feelings for you, which is a good thing. And I'm glad you expressed them. I thought some of your language was a little strong,[15] but I was happy to see how passionate you were about the subject."

"So do I get an A?" I asked.

---

15. Probably the blenders.

"Unfortunately, I'm going to have to give you an incomplete."

"Why?"

Then he said, "Because you didn't do the assignment, Harper." Then he started saying some bullshit about how, even though I don't support FGM, I was asked to "use anthropological arguments to make a theoretical case for it."

But I started to get really pissed off. Because I knew what this was about. This was about him not liking me. It's why he didn't call on me in class. It's why he never made eye contact with me. It's why he fucking *gushed* over Steinwhore and some of the other bitchy shit-nosers in class.

I didn't want him to get away with giving me an incomplete just because he didn't like me. So I asked him, "Why don't you ever call on me in class?"

And he said, "You're right to think that I call on you less frequently than some of the other students. But that's because you often don't contribute positively to conversations, Harper.[16] You like to yell about your opinion instead of contributing to a thoughtful dialogue."

But I knew that was bullshit, so I told him, "I think you don't call on me because you don't think I'm pretty."

And he looked kind of shocked. He said, "What?"

So I looked at him right in the eye[17] and asked him, "Mr. Doe, do you think I'm pretty?"

---

16. Fuck you, Mr. Doe!
17. I couldn't believe how brave I was.

And you know what he said? "I think you're a very lovely young lady, but you need to learn how to control your impulses, Harper."

I fucking knew it. *A lovely lady!* Suddenly it all made sense to me.

Mr. Doe had a crush on me. That's why he never made eye contact with me and why he was always flirting with Sarah Stein. It was because he thought Sarah Stein was an unattractive whore[18] and thought *I* was the hot one. I fucking knew it!

After we spoke, he thanked me for staying late and asked me to consider rewriting the paper. Then he got kind of awkward and said, "Have a good week, Harper."

I walked home kind of confused. I had all these strange thoughts circulating around inside my head.

I mean, I actually did think Mr. Doe was hot. He seemed so smart and sure about himself and I thought it was hot. He knew about so many things and had so much energy and seemed so nice and probably gentle and caring. He probably would never ask anyone to cut their vaginas and he would probably be so sweet and soft and nothing like the African guys. I thought about maybe having sex with him[19] to lose my virginity. Because he'd probably know how to do it really good since he knows about everything and every culture.

---

18. Which he'd be right about.
19. I think I'd probably be good at sex because my mom always said I have a "dancer's body."

And I know this sounds crazy, but then I started thinking that maybe I would accidentally get pregnant with his baby and then he'd be stuck with me forever, but in a good way, like we'd have to get married. And then we could fuck all we want because we'd be married. And after I get menopause and can't have babies anymore, we would fuck even more because there'd be no chance of getting pregnant or AIDS. And we would be married and have a nice family and he would teach me about the world and we'd die together and share the same coffin because it would be more romantic that way.[20]

And when I got home, I told Slutnick about my amazing meeting with Mr. Doe. But Slutnick didn't think it was amazing at all. She was shocked when I told her that he called me a "lovely lady."

She said, "Harper, don't you think that's kind of strange?"

And I said, "No, it was really nice." And then I told Slutnick how I was thinking about fucking him and that I thought he might want to because he had a huge crush on me. And SN was even more shocked.

She said, "Harper, I think you have to report this guy. I think this counts as harassment."

I told Slutnick that she was probably just jealous. But Slutnick said that it's really important to report any kind of "over-the-line" behavior from teachers.

---

20. Okay, I know this sounds corny and crazy but, Miss Rita, my mind was going a million miles a minute!

Suddenly, I got so embarrassed. What if Mr. Doe really *did* step over the line? What if I really *was* victim of sexual harassment?[21]

Miss Rita!

And then I got super embarrassed. And Slutnick said, "Are you okay, Harper? Your face is totally flushed."

And she was right. I felt my cheeks and they were burning. And my ears were hot, which is something that happens when I get super nervous.

I don't know what to do, Miss Rita. I feel so dirty right now. What if Slutnick is right and I *was* sexually harassed? What should I do? What if I report Mr. Doe and he gets arrested and goes to jail and I lose my chance to marry him and have his babies and lose my virginity for the first time? I feel like I might be in love with my abuser, which is what happens in these kinds of relationships.[22]

I feel all these weird feelings at the same time and I don't know how to think about anything right now!

Please help me!

Harper Jablonski

---

21. Okay, I know I wasn't raped or anything, but maybe harassment starts with "lovely lady" and ends with me tied to a bedpost getting my vagina cut off!

22. I don't want to become a statistic.

November 23

Dear Miss Rita,

I'm writing to tell you that I'm never going to write to you again.[1]&[2]

This has been a very strange week for me.[3]

First of all, I want to thank you for coming to visit me. When I first saw you, sitting on the bench outside my dorm room, I was so confused. To be honest, I didn't recognize you at first because you'd gotten a little fat[4] in your face and you cut your hair so short, like an old woman.

And then when you said, "Harper," I looked at you and saw your eyes, which hadn't changed at all. It's weird how a person's eyes can stay exactly the same even if the face around them gets older and fatter.

Once I realized it was you, Miss Rita, a wave of hot flashed through my body because I suddenly realized that you had come all the way to St. Louis just to visit me. And it made me feel so nice and so loved.

And when I asked what you were doing here, you said, "I just thought you could use some company, Harper," and that

---

1. Which maybe you're happy about. ;-)
2. Ironic, right?
3. Okay, I know I always say that but this week in particular was really really weird.
4. Sorry! But you had.

made me want to cry because it was such a nice thing to say because I knew you were trying to not make a big deal out of coming to visit.[5]

And it made me feel so emotional! And that's why I didn't say anything to you. Because I thought, if I said even one word, I would start to sob immediately, so I just tried to not say anything.

And then you suggested we should get some coffee at Starbucks to "talk things through," and I didn't know what you meant, but I was feeling SO great, just being near you.

And I know this is going to sound weird but, on the walk to Starbucks, I actually started picturing you as my mother. I don't know if you could tell but I was sneaking little looks at your face to see if there were any similarities to my face.[6]

I can't even remember what you were saying on the walk because every thought was in my head! I started thinking about how you got to St. Louis. That you had to fly from New York and rent a car and get a hotel room, and I was thinking how amazing it was that you did all that for me, Miss Rita. No one ever did anything so nice for me I think.

---

5. It's like when people make donations under the name "Anonymous." If I made a donation, I would definitely put my full name so people knew I had done it, but it's nicer if you don't.
6. And there actually were. You have a lot of blackheads on your forehead and the beginnings of female balding, but otherwise I think we could totally be related.

And when we got to Starbucks, I was so looking forward to our conversation. It felt like I was in a dream because sometimes, when I write letters to you, I picture you reading them and nodding and understanding and laughing.[7]

So I was thinking that talking to you would be like writing you a letter but to your actual face, which was such a weird but wonderful thing to think about.

And I was imagining all the things we could talk about and how I could get your advice about everything going on in my life[8] and how you would make things that seemed like *big* problems seem like *small* problems or like *not* problems at all and then you would tell me that I "deserve to be happy" and we would just stare into each other's eyes[9] and smile and then I would go back home to Slutnick and you would go back home to New York and we'd both feel happy.

But, Miss Rita, I have to say that right now, I'm kind of in the mindset that you're a massive tool and, I'm sorry to say, but a bitchface as well.

You see, I was really looking forward to our conversation, but as soon as we sat down with our coffees, you suddenly got really serious and you looked at me like I was sick or something.[10]

---

7. Not *at* me, but like if I'm trying to be funny. ;-)
8. Like trying to make more friends who are like me or trying to lose my virginity or dealing with weird teachers or trying to not hate my parents because they're assholes.
9. But not like dykes.
10. Like I should be *pitied.*

And then you started saying things that, frankly, Miss Rita, made me feel really pissed off.

Like when you said I sounded "frequently unstable" in my letters and suggested I take "a little 'life break' for a while,"[11] I felt like you weren't my friend anymore. It felt like you were *judging* me or telling me what to do instead of *listening* to me.

And when you said that my last letter was really "alarming" because you thought I was wrongly accusing a teacher of something horrible.[12]

And then I wondered why you came all the way to St. Louis just to tell me I was insane.[13]

I know I write really crazy things to you, but a lot of times, I just get carried away because that's what it feels like to be inside of my mind. I have the craziest thoughts in my head sometimes and it's hard to express them through regular, casual words.[14]

---

11. Which sounds like something you say to someone when you want them to a) kill themselves, or b) go away to a mental ward.

12. Obviously, I wasn't going to turn him in, Miss R. I'm not a fucking moron.

13. And then I started thinking AGAIN about the flight you had to take and the hotel room and the rental car. Except NOW I was thinking about them in a different way, like WHY would you get all that shit just to come here and insult me?

14. Like sometimes I feel upset and it feels like I want to die so I'll say, "I want to die, Miss Rita!!!" which sounds to you probably like I'm going to kill myself. But really, what I mean is that I *want* to die. Which is a real thought in that moment, but it doesn't mean I'm *actually* going to kill myself. You have to learn to read between the lines better, Miss R.

But that doesn't mean that I'm "unstable" or need a "life break."

And that's why I basically said nothing the whole time. That's why I just nodded and walked back to my dorm alone. That's why I basically didn't even smile once at you or thank you for coming to visit me.

SO.

I think it's probably best if we don't write to each other for a while because, Miss Rita, I think I probably use you for a crutch. And I know it's sometimes really hard to live without a crutch, especially when you feel like your legs really hurt, but it's better in the long run.[15]

---

15. Did I ever tell you about the time I had to go to Camp Firewood? Oh my fucking god, Miss Rita. In sixth grade, our school had to go on a weeklong camping trip. And I had never even had a *sleepover*, let alone a *week* of camping. I was totally freaked out about it, obviously. And the night before the trip, I basically had a breakdown and begged my mom to not make me go to Camp Firewood! I was just praying I got sick the night before so I could get out of it. (In fact, I even went to sleep in all of my clothing, hoping to overheat in the middle of the night and get sick. But I just got really sweaty and not sick.)

Anyway. My mom drove me to school in the morning, where there was a line of school buses waiting to take us up to Camp Firewood for the week. And I got so fucking panicked when I saw the buses because it suddenly made the trip *real.*

And I got on the bus and found a seat near the back and was trying to hold it together, but it was so hard to not cry. And then I saw my mother outside the window, getting back into her car to go back home.

cont.

And she waved at me and then I just fucking lost it. I broke down crying ON THE BUS with EVERYONE looking at me.

It was so fucking embarrassing, but I couldn't stop blubbering. It was like a civil rights hose of tears and snot, just *gushing* from my face. And my mother saw me and came on the bus.

So now, I was hysterically crying AND my mother was on the bus, so as you could imagine, it was embarrassing as fuck. And my mother walked to the back, where I was sitting (literally everyone was staring at me), and said, "Jesus, Harper. What's going on?" And I didn't know what to say because what I *wanted* to say was "Please take me home, Mom! I can't go away for a whole week with these people! I am so fucking homesick already and we haven't even left! Please please please don't make me go!"

But because I was so flustered, I ended up saying, "Mom, I forgot to pack shampoo." (Which was true, I did forget to bring shampoo, but that wasn't the reason I was crying.) And my mom said, "You could just use a bar of soap to wash your hair." And I said, "Really?" And she said, "Yes, just make a lather and use it like you would use regular shampoo." And I said, "Isn't it too drying?" And Mom said, "Well, you shouldn't use it every day, but one week is not going to damage your hair." And I said, "Thanks, Mom," and I calmed down a little bit. And then my mom walked off the bus. And I sat down. And literally no one said anything to me. Everyone on the bus heard this bizarre conversation about using bar soap as shampoo between the crying girl and her mother and no one said a word about it. The whole three-hour bus ride was SILENT.

But on that bus ride up to Camp Firewood, something changed in me, Miss Rita. I was calmer but not because my mom came on the bus and not because I wasn't worried about shampooing my hair. I was calmer because I realized something new about the world. I realized that I would be able to live in the world and that I would be okay on my

cont.

Also, I think you have a limited perspective in some ways, Miss Rita, and I don't really want your advice anymore.

Anyway, I hope you got home safely.

So long for now . . .

Harper Jablonski

———————

own. You know? Like I didn't bring shampoo, but I was able to make a little adjustment and use what I *did* bring.

And most of the time, I forget that I have that power and I go a little crazy and get really upset or angry.

But sometimes, when I'm in the shower, I'll make a lather from the bar of soap and use it as shampoo (and then use a ton of conditioner, obviously).

And so, even though I really appreciate everything you've done for me, I do think it's probably best for me to try washing my own hair for a while, even if it's with soap.

V.
DATING

A POST-GENDER-NORMATIVE MAN TRIES TO PICK UP A WOMAN AT A BAR

Hey, how's it going? Mind if I sidle up? I saw you over here sitting alone and I thought, "That's fine." A woman should be able to self-sustain. In fact a lot of women are choosing to stay alone, what with advances in salary equitability and maternity extensions, and I think it's an important and compelling trend.

I noticed that you were about to finish your drink and I was wondering if I could possibly watch you purchase another one. And, at the risk of being forward, if you would consider purchasing one for me.

What do you do? And before you answer, I'm not looking for a necessarily work-related response. I don't think we have to be defined by our industrial pursuits, especially when they're antiquated and heteronormative. I curse my mother, who is an otherwise lovely human person, for not buying me an Easy-Bake Oven when I was younger. I grew up idolizing male thugs like Neil Armstrong and Jimmy Carter. And, yes, I work at ESPN, but I spend more time being spiritual and overcoming adversity, for example, than I do working for some faceless corporation. And if I were to find a mate, be it you or someone else here tonight, I would be more than happy to tell the proverbial "man" that I quit so I can raise our offspring with gender-neutral hobbies, while my biologically female partner continues to pursue her interests, be they industrial, recreational, or, yes, even sexual with another mate.

Oh, how gauche of me! I've just been chattering away incessantly like some kind of boy or girl who talks a lot. I haven't even properly introduced myself. Although, one often gets the uneasy sense that patriarchy dictates a learned and ultimately damaging order of events with men taking an unearned lead. My name is Terri, with a heart over the *i* instead of a dot. I have a heart, is what that says, and I'm not afraid to wear it on my sleeve.

So what do you think? Would you like to take me up on my offer for you to buy me that drink?

If you would like to respond, that would be wonderful. Of course, if you would like to continue to sit here silently, staring at me with that powerful gaze, which both breaks gender constructs and also scares me a bit, that would be fine as well.

What's that? I should go fuck myself? I agree! Men should be more self-generative! Thank you for your astute assertion. Why should women exclusively have to bear the burden of childbirth, when men are biologically doomed to fear commitment? It's counterintuitive and socially degrading.

Ahh, that beer is refreshing! Thank you for throwing it in my face on this warm summer evening.

Okay, okay! I'm leaving!

Thank you for your blunt rejection of me. It takes a lot of courage, which you no doubt have in equal measure to any other human. Now, if you'll excuse me, I'm going to the bathroom where I'll cry silently in a stall, questioning my body and texting my mom, but for now, I thank you for your time, which was equal in value to mine.

A POST-GENDER-NORMATIVE WOMAN TRIES TO PICK UP A MAN AT A BAR

Hey, how's it going? No, don't get up; I'll stand.

I saw you over here sitting alone and I thought, "How sad. A man shouldn't be left to drink all by himself. It's hard enough as it is with social pressures to conform to an unattainable idea of masculinity perpetuated by a patriarchal and antiquated set of phallocratic norms."

I noticed that you were about to finish that drink and I was wondering if I could buy you another one. I have a tab here. They know me. I drink pretty heavily.

I've been pounding Irish Car Bombs all night, but I'm willing to transition to cosmos if you're more inclined.

In fact, a cosmo may be a better option for me anyhow. Not because of its pink hue and dainty lemon rind, but because the alcohol content is lower and I have to be up fairly early for my corporate executive office job.

I'm not sure about your schedule for tomorrow morning— you could be doing anything from packing school lunches to midwifery—but I have to be up at 6:30 sharp. Mainly to hit the gym. And not because I'm concerned with maintaining a taut feminine physique but because the morning adrenaline rush gets my head in the corporate game. It's a minefield out there and the gym turns me into an emotional tank.

I should probably mention that I approached you with the sole intention of having sex with you. Ideally tonight. I assessed your body from the other end of the bar and thought that, irrespective of your personality, I'd like to have sex with you. I know we've only just met, but I enjoy being penetrated by a stranger with no promise of an emotional commitment. Call me old-fashioned.

Oh, how gauche of me! I've just been rambling on like some kind of Chatty Calvin. I haven't even properly introduced myself. My name is Terri, with a dollar sign over the *i*. I'm not afraid to make money, is what that says, especially if it's apportioned based on my physical efforts and intellectual abilities.

So what do you think? Would you like to take me up on my offer to buy you that drink? No? What about the indiscriminate sex? We could head back to my place, which is actually pretty dirty at the moment. It's really more of a crash pad. A landing spot for me and my Steelers-themed minifridge filled with domestic beer.

What's that? I'm harassing you? How horrible. And you probably won't even report it. All too often, men won't report harassment or abuse because it conflicts with an archaic sense of misguided masculinity and pride. But it's so important to alert the authorities of any aggressive behavior from a woman as soon as possible. A friendly tap on the shoulder becomes a less-than-playful nudge becomes throwing a man down two flights of stairs at three in the morning.

I'm just saying: Women Are Dangerous.

No, no! Don't call the bartender, he's been on his feet all day. I'll just leave.

No, no! Don't get the door, I'm perfectly capable of letting myself out.

And don't worry about me. I'm just going to head home, eat a TV dinner, and fall asleep in shapeless pajamas. But for now, I thank you for your time, which was roughly two-thirds as valuable as mine.

A GUY ON ACID TRIES
TO PICK UP A WOMAN
AT A BAR

Hey, how's it going? Mind if I sidle up? I saw you over here sitting alone and I started crying. In a way, we're all alone, but to be alone at a *bar*, at a place specifically designed to meet other humans—and what are humans? We're all just carbon-based light refractions anyway—was particularly unnerving. Do you want a piece of gum? I have four left.

Are you waiting for someone? It's always so awkward to approach a person at a bar and then find out they're waiting for someone else. I was waiting for someone tonight as well, but she never showed. It was my mother, who died in a car accident when I was seven.

She's not really dead. I just lied to you because I'm in denial because she actually is dead. It's like when the baby panda is torn away from its mother by a scientist. But I'm the baby panda and my mother is the mother panda and the scientist is my mother's faulty brake pads. Have you ever watched baseball? Do you know how to make fire? I would die in the wild! Do you want some gum? There's still three pieces left.

So, do you want to go out with me? Just kidding, we're already here. We're out. What is *out*? We're all carbon based! Do you want to have sex with me is what I really meant to ask you. Do you? I mean, not *here* of course, it would be gauche and my mother could walk in at any moment, but we could go back to my apartment, which smells because I rarely flush the toilet because I think I'm conserving water. But I flushed it before I came here in anticipation of meeting someone like you who would be disgusted by something like that. There's only two pieces of gum left! Time is running out on this gum! We'll all be dead in a hundred years!

What are you drinking? It's so weird how people drink alcohol at these places so that they can talk to each other. Alcohol is poison, you know. It's all poison, made from rotting fruits and vegetables. Isn't that so weird? And then we get in our cars and drive home! What a great idea: *Hey, let me sit inside this glass-and-metal death cage and drive it sixty miles an hour in the dark! It's not like I have a son who needs me!*

You have really beautiful eyes, by the way. The way the light in your stroma scatters across your ocular fluid creating a bluish-green color is attractive to me for some reason. I also like your body. Your cleavage excites me on a carnal, albeit unsustainable, level and the fact that you're revealing your legs in that short skirt makes me feel like you're eager to have sex with someone, which I also am. Even though I know you're mostly carbon based and that we share most of the same chemical compounds and we're all just light refractions through space, I still want to have sex with you. And even though I know you're almost genetically identical to the woman at the far end of the bar with the slight overbite, I still want to have sex with you a lot more than I want to have sex with her.

What's that? Your boyfriend just showed up? Oh yes, I can see why you'd prefer to date him. He is better looking than me. I'm ashamed of my physical body. I have a weird-looking sternum, but his looks more desirable. Does he make fire? Would he like my final piece of gum?

Ah yes! The sensation my face feels from you throwing your beer all over it is simply exhilarating! Thank you for enlivening my nervous system at this late hour.

Ow! Thank you, sir, for punching me in the face to defend your girlfriend from my frantic advances. The blood is now rushing to my face in a desperate attempt to stave off the pain and my prefrontal cortex is making a mental note to avoid carbon-based life-forms with your properly aligned sternum.

Okay, okay! I'm leaving!

If you see my mother, please tell her I'm in the bathroom wiping my face and nursing my wounds. And if the girl with the overbite appears to be leaving, tell her to wait a few minutes for me because I'd still be up for sex. Have a good night, which is just an arbitrary illusion created by the Earth blocking the sun.

A LIFELONG TEETOTALER, EMBARRASSED BY HIS OWN SOBRIETY, TRIES TO PICK UP A WOMAN AT A BAR

Hey, how's it going? Mind if I sidle up? I saw you over here drinking alone and I thought, "Awesome. I love alcohol. Love that stuff."

What are you drinking there? Just straight-up alcohol? Cool. That's how I like it too. Straight up. Or straight down. Just so long as it's alcohol, right?

Me? I'm nursing a ginger ale for now. Kind of the calm before the storm. The *alcohol* storm, that is. I'm definitely going to drink some alcohol in a bit, just layin' down the groundwork for some pretty serious imbibing.

What brings you in here? Probably the full bar, right? They have all different kinds of alcohol in here, which is so cool. I used to find it overwhelming, the amount of different alcohol drinks, but I just liquor it up so much that I'm able to try all the different kinds. Vodka's probably my favorite. But I also like rum, which is another kind of alcohol and which is made from sugarcane, which is cool.

So...

Did you see the ad for that new vodka? It looks like it's gonna be great. Looks like it might be stronger than the old stuff, which is awesome. Fingers crossed, right? Everyone in the commercial looks like they're having so much fun, which they should be—they're drinking alcohol. And at the end they say, "Drink responsibly." Which, in my world, translates to "Drink every day!"

Cool...

My tolerance is so high right now.

So I did a little research and there seems to be a controversy about where and when vodka—which derives from the diminutive of the Old Church Slavonic word for "water," *voda*—was invented. Some say it was Russia in the ninth century, others claim Poland a century before. All I know is that when I booze up, I feel alive! That's right, I drink vodka all the time, I don't even *care* when it was invented. In fact, sometimes I think *I* would have invented it if it didn't exist. I mean all it takes is creating a mash from a carbohydrate, adding yeast and distilling it in a boiling chamber, meting out the methanol, and then filtering and diluting it. And then, of course, the best part: the drinking!

But apparently during the communist period, vodka was rationed, which must have sucked. I would have been the guy with the hollow heel. You know what I'm talking about!

Yeah, I've been hittin' the bottle for a long time. Probably cigarettes too, who knows. I think I pounded my first drink when I was like twelve, whatever. I just love being drunk and drinking.

I am so wasted sometimes.

So, what do you think? Should we go back to my place to continue drinking alcohol together? I could show you my Periodic Table of Alcohol, which is a large chart that I made that ranks each kind of alcohol according to its Alcohol Content by Volume, starting with Mild Ciders and ending with Rectified Spirits.

No? Not into that? What about going to a park and drinking alcohol? No? How about going to your place where we can drink alcohol with an eye toward having sex with each other. Buyer beware, though, I will attempt to pour alcohol on your body and drink it off during the sex. Not because I find that kind of thing arousing, but because I don't like to spend any time or any activity not consuming, in some way, alcohol.

Ah! Thank you for throwing that alcohol in my face. It allows me to ingest it more quickly because you've thrown it with a speed and force that makes it enter my mouth faster than it would were I to drink it in a more traditional way. If you'll excuse me, though, I'm just going to run to the bathroom because I have to wash it out of my mouth. I mean "wash it out of my mouth" in an attempt to cleanse the palate for more alcohol! Which I love drinking.

But before I go, I'll just order one last drink. Hey, barkeep! Another ice water please! He knows what I mean. "Ice" is code for "vodka" and "water" is code for—you guessed it—"more vodka." He'll hook me up. He's a friend. On account of me being here so frequently and drinking alcohol.

Have a good evening, which can only be made better by drinking alcohol, something I've actually done and plan on continuing to actually do.

VI.
SPORTS

MARV ALBERT
IS MY THERAPIST

ME: Hi, Dr. Albert.

MARV ALBERT: A play-off atmosphere in here tonight!

ME: Well, it's been a tough week. My mother came to visit me.

MARV ALBERT: From downtown!

ME: And, of course, she immediately asked if I was still sleeping with Sarah.

MARV ALBERT: Out of bounds!

ME: Exactly. It's not her business.

MARV ALBERT: Unbelievable!

ME: And Sarah won't even return my calls.

MARV ALBERT: Rejected!

ME: I called her like twelve times last night.

MARV ALBERT: A dozen! Unanswered!

ME: I don't know why I'm surprised. We haven't been intimate in months.

MARV ALBERT: Stuck outside the perimeter.

ME: Yeah.

MARV ALBERT: Unable to penetrate!

ME: I guess.

MARV ALBERT: Just can't find the hole!

ME: That's a little crass, but yeah. Anyway, I actually met this other girl, Becky.

MARV ALBERT: A clutch rebound!

ME: She's a waitress.

MARV ALBERT: Another easy opportunity!

ME: She's just coming out of a messy divorce.

MARV ALBERT: A layup!

ME: And she said she hasn't been on a date in years.

MARV ALBERT: Uncontested!

ME: Everything seemed to be going pretty well. I took her back to my apartment.

MARV ALBERT: Off to a great start—

ME: We were on the bed—

MARV ALBERT: Great hands!

ME: Thanks, Dr. Albert, but she suddenly got like freaked out and made some weird excuse—

MARV ALBERT: An explosion of emotions!

ME: Yeah!

MARV ALBERT: Pandemonium!

ME: Right. For no reason.

MARV ALBERT: No choice but to foul!

ME: What?

MARV ALBERT: You've got to foul!

ME: What are you suggesting?

MARV ALBERT: With the game on the line, you have to foul!

ME: I would never hurt her.

MARV ALBERT: Then that's the ball game.

ME: Yeah, she threw on her jacket and ran out.

MARV ALBERT: Traveling!

ME: So I called after her!

MARV ALBERT: Called for traveling!

ME: But she left me there, stunned—

MARV ALBERT: Unable to recover!

ME: So I tried to run after her.

MARV ALBERT: Trying to stop a breakaway!

ME: But she slammed the door in my face.

MARV ALBERT: Stuffed!

ME: So I'm standing there alone in my apartment—

MARV ALBERT: Just letting the clock expire!

ME: And then, of course, I started feeling terrible about Sarah again.

MARV ALBERT: Back-to-back losses at home.

ME: Do you think I'll ever get over her?

MARV ALBERT: And now a quick word from our sponsor.

ME: What?

MARV ALBERT: Visit your local Ford dealer to check out the new Ford SUV, the Ford Flex.

ME: I can't afford a car right now.

MARV ALBERT: It's the best in its class.

ME: I was never the best in my class.

MARV ALBERT: Have you driven a Ford lately?

ME: I can't drive.

MARV ALBERT: And we're back!

ME: I've been sitting here the whole time.

MARV ALBERT: Refusing to go away!

ME: Well, I've paid for the whole hour.

MARV ALBERT: We're going to overtime!

ME: We are?

MARV ALBERT: Yes!

ME: Will I be charged?

MARV ALBERT: Yes!

ME: How much?

MARV ALBERT: Double.

ME: Double?

MARV ALBERT: Triple.

ME: Triple?

MARV ALBERT: Triple-double!

ME: Did my insurance say they would cover it?

MARV ALBERT: Rejected!

ME: I figured.

MARV ALBERT: Time for one more!

ME: Dr. Albert, I feel like I have nothing left to live for.

MARV ALBERT: Things are not looking good!

ME: Sometimes I feel like I should just throw myself out the window.

MARV ALBERT: A jumper from the top of the key!

ME: I feel like it's the only solution.

MARV ALBERT: A quick fadeaway!

ME: Exactly!

MARV ALBERT: A dagger!

ME: A dagger?

MARV ALBERT: Straight down the middle!

ME: Seems a little bloody—

MARV ALBERT: A bullet!

ME: A bullet?

MARV ALBERT: A high-percentage shot!

ME: That is tempting.

MARV ALBERT: One shot could end this whole thing!

ME: It would be so simple.

MARV ALBERT: A solid execution!

ME: Okay, I'll do it.

MARV ALBERT: Not in my house!

ME: No one would even miss me.

MARV ALBERT: An easy loss to get over!

ME: The world would be better off without me, right, Dr. Albert?

MARV ALBERT: Yes! And it counts!

CARMELO ANTHONY AND I DEBRIEF OUR FRIENDS AFTER A PICKUP GAME AT THE YMCA

ME: Hey, guys! Sorry I'm late.

> CARMELO ANTHONY: Hey, guys. Sorry I'm late.

ME: The most amazing thing just happened!

> CARMELO ANTHONY: The most annoying thing just happened.

ME: I was at the YMCA, just shooting around . . .

> CARMELO ANTHONY: I got stuck at the Y again.

ME: . . . and guess who's shooting *right* next to me?

> CARMELO ANTHONY: Some skinny white dude was lobbing air balls right next to me.

ME: Carmelo Anthony! Melo Yellow himself! I couldn't believe it. I've always been a die-hard fan.

CARMELO ANTHONY: Probably one of these guys who comes to two games a year and calls himself a die-hard fan.

ME: I even went to those two games this year. So I just played it cool, kept to myself, did my thing.

CARMELO ANTHONY: He kept shooting these ridiculous half-court shots to get my attention.

ME: And I glanced over at him.

CARMELO ANTHONY: He was staring at me the whole time.

ME: And it seemed like he wanted some company.

CARMELO ANTHONY: I just wanted to be left alone.

ME: So I walked up to him and was like, "Hey, Melo, how 'bout a little one-on-one."

CARMELO ANTHONY: He was like (*affecting a loser's voice*), "Uh . . . Mr. Anthony, I'm such a huge fan."

ME: And Melo was like, "You think you can take me?"

CARMELO ANTHONY: And I was like, "I guess we can shoot around for a minute."

ME: So I said, "It's on." Can you believe I said that? "It's on."

CARMELO ANTHONY: He said (*affecting a girlish falsetto*), "Thank you so much, Mr. Anthony! It's such an honor! My friends are never gonna believe me."

ME: So I suggested we play shirts and skins.

> CARMELO ANTHONY: I guess he thought we were actually playing a real game.

ME: You know, just in case more guys jumped in.

> CARMELO ANTHONY: And before I could tell him that there's no way I was playing skins.

ME: I took my shirt off.

> CARMELO ANTHONY: I almost threw up.

ME: And I've really filled out the last few months. I've been doing tons of crunches.

> CARMELO ANTHONY: He looked like one of those kids in a Sally Struthers commercial.

ME: I'm kind of ripped. I actually think he was a little shocked.

> CARMELO ANTHONY: It was actually kind of shocking the way you could see every single one of his ribs.

ME: So I took the ball out.

> CARMELO ANTHONY: I let him start with the ball.

ME: And I tried to drive by him.

> CARMELO ANTHONY: I think he was trying to dribble past me.

ME: But he was quick.

> CARMELO ANTHONY: I literally did not move my feet.

ME: And he blocked me!

CARMELO ANTHONY: I barely raised my hand and he kind of just ran into it.

ME: And Melo was like, "Not in my house!"

CARMELO ANTHONY: And I think I apologized to him. Like just instinctively. Like when you step on a cat's tail and you're like, "Oh! Sorry, cat!"

ME: But we were both totally in the zone.

CARMELO ANTHONY: While he was prancing around, I finally finished reading that *Economist* article you emailed me.

ME: It was like we were the only two people on the planet.

CARMELO ANTHONY: It's really terrible how they're exploiting those Nicaraguan coffee farmers.

ME: I don't think he's really been tested in a while.

CARMELO ANTHONY: So I decided to give him the ball. Just to get it over with.

ME: But I robbed him in the paint and did one of my moves.

CARMELO ANTHONY: He kept trying to dribble the ball between his legs.

ME: I did my Harden Eurostep, my Rondo No-Look, my J-Craw Step Back.

CARMELO ANTHONY: But it just bounced off his knee, out of bounds. It was so embarrassing.

ME: It was so *empowering*! I hadn't played like that since high school.

CARMELO ANTHONY: He's clearly never played against another actual human person. And the worst part was . . .

ME: Oh! I forgot about the best part!

CARMELO ANTHONY: . . . there was this woman teaching a yoga class nearby and the ball kept flying over to her.

ME: There was this yoga chick near us and she was like *eyeing* me the whole time.

CARMELO ANTHONY: I could tell she wanted to kill this guy every time she brought the ball back to us.

ME: She was totally into me, like bringing the ball back for me . . .

CARMELO ANTHONY: And then he actually started trash-talking. Have you ever heard a skinny white dude try to talk trash?

ME: We were both getting a little dirty in the mouth.

CARMELO ANTHONY: It was like watching a Chihuahua bark at a hydrant.

ME: I was like, "I'm gonna beat you like a redheaded stepchild!"

CARMELO ANTHONY: He said something horrifying about child abuse.

ME: And he was clearly intimidated.

CARMELO ANTHONY: I was actually kind of scared. He seemed crazed.

ME: So then I said, "Hope you brought toast, Melo, 'cause I'm about to spread my *jam* all over you!"

> CARMELO ANTHONY: Then he said something kind of gross, so I just kept my mouth shut.

ME: He was speechless!

> CARMELO ANTHONY: And people were starting to notice us so I said, "Next point wins."

ME: I think I must have wore him down 'cause he was like, "Sorry, brother, I only got one more left."

> CARMELO ANTHONY: So I gave him the ball.

ME: So I grabbed the rock.

> CARMELO ANTHONY: And he started dribbling it the wrong way.

ME: I went to my sweet spot.

> CARMELO ANTHONY: Then he turned around and heaved it from half-court.

ME: And I launched a bullet from the fifty!

> CARMELO ANTHONY: But the ball was heading nowhere near the basket.

ME: It was heading right toward that sweet nylon hole.

> CARMELO ANTHONY: And I could tell that it was gonna slam off the backboard and right into yoga girl again.

ME: And I could tell that yoga girl was watching.

> CARMELO ANTHONY: So I did the only thing any sane person would do.

ME: And then Melo did the stupidest thing.

CARMELO ANTHONY: I jumped up and grabbed the ball.

ME: He goal-tended my shot!

CARMELO ANTHONY: And I softly tipped the ball in, winning the game and, frankly, saving that girl's life.

ME: And then he acted like *he* won the game!

CARMELO ANTHONY: But the guy was acting like *he* won the game!

ME: But I didn't want to call him out. I mean, it was just a friendly game.

CARMELO ANTHONY: You know, it was always kind of annoying to work out at the Y, but this was more than I could take.

ME: I think this might be the beginning of a pretty heated rivalry.

CARMELO ANTHONY: I just hope I never see him again.

ME: It'll probably become a regular thing for us.

CARMELO ANTHONY: I canceled my membership on the way out.

ME: This is why New York City is the greatest city in the world.

CARMELO ANTHONY: This is why I gotta leave New York.

ME: You run into the coolest people.

CARMELO ANTHONY: You're accosted by the weirdest people.

ME: But what I realized is . . .

CARMELO ANTHONY: Anybody can be delusional and dangerous.

ME: . . . everyone is just as normal as I am.

A MARRIAGE COUNSELOR TRIES TO HECKLE AT A KNICKS GAME

Let's go Knicks!!! But let's also recognize the positive attributes of the opposing team!!!

Come on, Knicks!! But please note that I'm supporting the Knicks because I live in the same city as the team's arena, which is a distinction as arbitrary as what players are assigned to what team!!! That is, I could just as easily be supporting the other team were I to live in their arena's city!!!

Melo, you suck! And in some cultures you would be revered for such behavior! The Yanomami tribe, for example, will affect a sucking motion to indicate safe passage to a neighboring tribe!!!

Ref, are you blind?! If so, it would be amazing that you've been so accurately officiating up until this last play, which, for vantage reasons, appeared to me to be called incorrectly!!!

Of course, I'm judging this as a layman and you have a far more appropriate view to fully evaluate what just occurred!! I honor your craft and insight and, in a way, I *value* your incorrect calls! It means you're human, and that's healthy!! Feel good about yourself and, in moments like this, remember how many calls you got right!! The world is complicated!

DEFENSE! DEFENSE! But also, OFFENSE! OFFENSE! Lest we forget how quickly the offense becomes the defense! These frameworks are constantly in flux!!!

FOUL?! Are you kidding me?! If you are, I will say, simply, thank you! Laughter and joke telling are healthy and can be used to convey messages that may otherwise be too difficult to express!

Get your head out of your ass, you must be the most flexible person I've ever seen!!!

Go for a three!!! I want to see this game go to overtime! I know it's difficult to hear, but I believe there is a future for you both!!! Right now, you're in the thick of it, you're blinded by anger, which is normal and understandable! Frankly, I'd be surprised if you *weren't* upset! The wounds haven't yet healed!

There were flagrant fouls, yes!! And there were missed opportunities!!! But there were good moments as well! The national anthem! The jump ball! The halftime show! These were good and *right* and real!! And to discount these good moments is as irresponsible as to count only the bad moments!!!

In fact, may you both win, regardless of the "score"!! What is a "score" anyway?! An arbitrary number assigned in accordance with how many times a ball goes through a hoop?! How silly compared to the amount of times you've overcome adversity together! Why don't we count those times?! Like when there was a loose ball, and everyone tried to pick it up, regardless of allegiance?! There were no "teams" then!! There were no egos! There was just a ball that needed picking up!

If we're going to count the "score," why not count smiles?! Or pats on the back?! Or simple gestures that tell the other person, "Hey, I get it"?!

What's that?! I'm being kicked out of the game?! Why?! What'd I do?!

I'm talking too much?! I'm being too loud and ruining the experience for those around me?!

Well, that's perfectly understandable! Here we are trying to enjoy a sporting event, and I'm distracting everyone with my misguided enthusiasm, unending commentary, and meticulous analyses that conflict with the spirit of the game!!!

I can totally understand where you guys are coming from and I will leave on my own accord! In fact, I thank you for your blunt dismissal of me! I don't think I deserve to explain my position as my actions have already indicated my lack of regard for the other fans, the teams, and, frankly, the sport at large!!!

Okay, okay, I'm leaving!!!

I hope you all enjoy the rest of the game!!! May the home team prevail! Or the visiting team! Or, if possible, may they both prevail by transcending the false notion of prevailing!!!

VII.
SELF-HELP

SMILING TRICKS YOUR BRAIN INTO THINKING IT'S HAPPY

When I was a little boy, my mother told me that if I feel sad, I should force myself to smile because it will trick my brain into thinking it's happy.

And she was right.

Now, whenever I feel sad, I just smile and suddenly, magically, I'm happy.

And I discovered that it's not just limited to happiness. I can convince myself of anything just by making a face that corresponds to the feeling I want to have. For example, when I'm tired, I make an energetic face and I immediately feel a surge of vitality. And when I'm feeling hungry, I make a bloated face like I just ate too much birthday cake and then my brain is tricked into thinking I'm stuffed to the gills!

Last month, I was really down in the dumps. My fiancée

left me for my boss, who then impregnated her and fired me. Needless to say, I was pretty depressed! So what did I do? That's right: I smiled and, although it took a few minutes, I eventually felt better.

But even though I felt better, I still had some problems. For example, after I lost my job, I couldn't pay my rent. But instead of feeling sorry for myself or frantically looking for a cheap sublet, I just made the face of someone who *had* paid their rent and, though it didn't happen right away, I started to feel like I actually *did* pay my rent. And you know what? I felt a whole lot better. My mother really was right! It felt great!

And although I was kicked out of my apartment for not actually paying my rent and I started living under the Verrazano Bridge, clutching a hobo and his pet rat for warmth, I just made the face of someone who was living in a big mansion with two swimming pools and my own helipad. And you know what happened? I started feeling like I was living in Beverly Hills, 90210! (I even made a face like I bought my mother a new car! And, judging from my face, she loved it!)

And when the scurvy set in due to a severe lack of vitamin C and I started gnawing on the hobo and his pet rat in an unconscious attempt to nourish myself, I just made the face of someone chewing on a fancy steak dinner with a heaping side of mashed potatoes. Yup, sometimes all you need is to believe and you could convince yourself of anything! They were delicious!

And my mother's advice really got me out of a bind when I started stalking my former boss and pregnant ex-fiancée. I would just make a very casual face of someone not stalking anybody while I waited outside their house. And when they left the house to go to dinner, I followed them in a car that I had hot-wired and stolen, careful to make the face of someone who would not hot-wire a car.

And then I waited outside the restaurant and, when they ordered dessert, I stuffed my hobo's pet rat inside a mason jar and threw it through the restaurant's window, shattering the glass and sending the hobo's rat scurrying through the restaurant, bloodied and frantic.

At this point, I made the face of someone who didn't do all of those things and I immediately relaxed. Yep, sometimes the simplest solutions are also the best!

Then, when the patrons started running out of the restaurant, I made the face of someone not tackling my former boss and pregnant ex-fiancée and not stabbing them all over their bodies with a shiv I made from gnawing on a metal spoon I stole from the hobo's pocket.

But what I didn't realize was that the hobo had followed me to the restaurant because I had stolen his pet rat and favorite spoon. What a crazy coincidence! But instead of getting flustered, I just calmly made the face of someone who was happy to see a vengeful hobo. And then I actually *felt* happy to see him. Crazy, right? Fake it till you make it!

And while I was making the face of someone not killing a hobo with his own spoon, I felt totally at ease!

And when the police arrested me, I just made the face of someone who definitely didn't murder my former boss, my pregnant ex-fiancée, and my new roommate, who was a schizophrenic hobo, and even though the police didn't believe me, my brain was tricked into thinking I was innocent and that felt great! I guess sometimes, if you tell yourself something, you really can believe it!

And throughout the trial I made the face of someone who didn't insist upon stroking my newly acquired pet rat on the defense stand. And when the jury read the guilty verdict, you know what I did? You got it! I smiled and thanked them for acquitting me and I actually started to feel like I *was* acquitted. Wow! It's like magic!

And as I was being marched to the electric chair, I made the face of a man who was being marched to Disneyland and then my brain *believed* it was going to Disneyland and I was so happy because I love Disneyland. And when they pulled the lever and forty thousand volts of electricity surged through my body, I made the face of someone who was riding Space Mountain. And I smiled and smiled and smiled!

I know it sounds totally corny, but sometimes all you need is a little faith.

IF SHE RAN INTO ME NOW . . .

If she ran into me now, she would definitely fall in love with me.

I mean, it would be a little difficult not to.

I am the best version of myself at this very moment, and if she saw me like this, if she saw me right now, she would fall in love with me, probably forever.

I did laundry this morning so my clothes smell good. But more than that, when I wash my jeans, when I wash *these* jeans, they look particularly good on me. But only on the day that I wash them. The fibers seem to coalesce, to tighten a bit, creating a more formal fit around my leg. But because they're blue jeans, it shows that I'm casual. Formal-fitting blue jeans: highbrow and lowbrow. She's gonna love that.

If she ran into me now, she would see my jeans and she would think: "He's a serious person."

If she ran into me now, she would see my arms, she would see the veins in my arms. I did a hundred push-ups this morning. Three sets of thirty-three. Which is only ninety-nine. So I do one more at the end, which I kind of half do, but it still counts. So the veins in my arms are protruding a bit more than usual. The veins look amazing, frankly. It's like right on the cusp of heroin addict. If she just saw my veins, she'd think I was a goddamn linebacker, frankly.

She'd probably notice my veins and think they're always like that, they're always protruding because I'm just naturally strong. I won't mention anything about the push-ups. Let my body speak for itself.

And I only drank stuff that would make me smell good. There was a fancy iced tea on sale this morning at the bodega. It had spearmint in it, so I smell like the spearmint. I think it was only a tertiary ingredient, but that's what makes it so perfect. If we ended up kissing tonight—and I don't mean to presume that that's what would definitely happen—but if we ended up kissing—and I don't want to rule that out—I'd taste just a little like spearmint. And she'd probably just think that's how I naturally taste.

She should be walking by any second. Any second now.

Yeah. I'll give it another few minutes.

If she ran into me now, we'd be together forever. If she could see me right at this moment, everything would make sense. She'd see I'm not the same silent loser from high school. The same little pipsqueak kid whose mother came early to every game and sat in the front row with her camcorder. She'd see I've grown up into a person, into a human being. And a pretty phenomenal human being.

I mean, look at how my day's gone. It's irresistible. If she met me exactly at this moment, she'd probably ask me what I was up to today and I would tell her the truth, which is so unbelievably interesting that she would be overwhelmed with adoration and we'd run off together and probably end up getting married pretty quickly. If she would just walk by! Jesus!

She'd probably ask me where I've just come from, what I'm doing uptown. And I'll tell her: "I was with my aunt. She's ninety-four and needs some company. So I was just hanging out with her and then I thought I'd sit in Central Park for a few minutes. My aunt's the coolest." Then I'd say, "She's kind of my best friend," pretending to be embarrassed at having a ninety-four-year-old best friend. She'd think it was sweet how I looked embarrassed and I'd shrug.

And she'll probably ask what I'm doing tonight. Once again, I'm in the perfect position to tell the truth. I got tickets to a Knicks game. That's too lowbrow for you? Well, I'm actually going with my friend who's a cultural anthropologist. That's the kind of people I hang out with. Now who's lowbrow? Knicks game, cultural anthropologist. Lowbrow, highbrow. I'm hard to pin down. I'm all over the map!

Where is she? I really thought she'd be coming by about now. I mean, I'm pretty sure she's in the city. Jerry mentioned that she'd be in the city this weekend. I'll wait a little bit more. She'll be here.

And when I see her, I'll act surprised and say hello and

then take the tiniest of pauses before I say her name to give her the impression that I was scrolling through a Rolodex of other names. "I've got a lot going on these days, you understand."

She'll probably ask me where I'm living. And, again, I'll just tell her the truth, which happens to be fucking awesome: I'm living in Queens.

Just moved there. If that doesn't seal the deal, I don't know what will. If that doesn't make her completely reevaluate me, I don't know what will. I mean, it's Queens! It's the most interesting of the boroughs. *What is it?* It's so mercurial! Queens!

If I lived around this area, in *Manhattan*, she'd think I'm stuffy and elitist. Manhattan! Like I've retired or something. Like I was given a golden parachute that I decided to land in the center of the universe. It's so obvious. *Manhattan.*

And the Bronx? The Bronx! It'd seem like I'm trying to make some kind of violent statement. Why would I live in the Bronx? Who am I trying to impress? What kind of battle did I lose in life to wind up in the Bronx?

And Staten Island? Telling her I moved to Staten Island? I may as well tell her I moved to Jupiter or Kansas, or I'm shooting myself in the face tonight because I have absolutely nothing left to live for and no one would give a shit if I suddenly fell off the face of the earth by moving to Staten Island!

And Brooklyn. Move to Brooklyn? That is the worst of the boroughs. It's such an awful borough that I'm embarrassed to live in Queens because it's also a borough and that tenuous association is enough to humiliate me. Brooklyn! Overtaken by hipsters with thick-framed prescription-less glasses and ironic banjos and graphic designers who work for Saatchi and Saatchi but call themselves postmodern artists. If there was a draft, and Brooklyn was in Canada, and I could either go to Brooklyn and be safe or Vietnam and be killed, I'd go to Vietnam and I'd gladly be shot down instead of going to that hellhole that God would forsake, except it would mean that He would have to step foot in Brooklyn!

But I'm in Queens. Queens. It's so perfectly diverse. Queens: *Who am I?* I can interact with anyone! That's what Queens says. I'm open-minded; *I don't see color.* She'd probably want to come over to my house. Just to *see* Queens. "Hey, can we go to a little midnight diner?" she'd probably ask. Sure, we can go to Astoria. There are little midnight diners on every corner. "Can we go dancing?" Absolutely. Let's go to Corona, there are Latin Quarters on every block. There are so many Latin Quarters in Corona, we call them Latin Dollars! That's a little joke we make in Queens. It's silly. It's a Queens joke. Wanna see a Mets game? Sure! Why don't you take a few more days before you gotta head back up to school and we'll stay in bed late and check out a Mets game together. We can eat a late breakfast at this little hole-in-the-wall where the Greek guy knows my name and we could rent bikes and head out to Citi Field and hold hands in the bleachers and she'll say something like, "These seats are actually amazing because you can see the whole park."

Jesus, what time is it?

I should probably just head home. Where is she? How could she not walk through Central Park? Who doesn't walk through Central Park when they're visiting their parents on spring break? Who doesn't think to do that?

This is the best park in the city. Maybe the state. I don't know. But this is definitely a good park. I mean, I don't think anyone would be disappointed by this park. I don't think anyone's ever walked out of Central Park and said, "Not For Me."

So I'm sure she'll probably amble through here in a bit. In high school, her parents were on Seventy-Ninth Street. I'm sure they're still there. So she'd most likely enter through that north gate. Unless they moved. I can't imagine they would have moved. Unless, with the economy and everything. But they probably paid off their apartment; people don't rent up here. They were pretty rich. She always dressed so nicely. Like everything was tattered, but it was somehow still nice. Her little woolen pea coat, her torn little woolen pea coat. She was able to make wool sexy somehow. She was able to bring out the animal side of the wool, which makes sense 'cause it's from an animal. But people don't do that with wool anymore. It's latex that's supposed to be sexy. Or spandex. Or something else totally unnatural. Not for me! I like what's real. I like what's honest. I like her. I'm sure she'll be here any second.

I'll just wait it out. I'll just be ready. That's all I can do. "When opportunity knocks, you gotta be ready." Who said that? I think it was my father. No, it must be somebody more famous. I think it's a famous quote. I must've paraphrased.

I can't imagine she's still dating that idiot, that abstract painter idiot. That couldn't possibly last. It was going nowhere. They both knew it. Last time I saw her, at that stupid party, she said, "He's sweet. You don't know him, he's actually really sweet." What the hell is "sweet"? I'm "sweet." Anybody could be "sweet"! That's literally the easiest thing to be to someone else. *Sweet.* What a douchebag loser idiot. *Sweet.* I suffer for my life! I suffer every day! And for what? To mean something! To contribute, which I plan on doing. But oh no! He's *sweet.* Go sell car insurance! *Sweet.* He should be shot and he knows it!

And what the hell am I doing here, letting all these people pass me by who aren't her! What the hell am I doing? Who are these idiots who aren't her, just passing me by! I'm being wasted on them! They don't care that I'm going to a Knicks game with an anthropologist! They don't care that I just came from my ninety-four-year-old aunt's house! They're not her! They don't care that my dark blue jeans are perfectly fitted right now and my veins are protruding in the best possible way. No! They're just going on with their dumb day like their lives are important, while I'm sitting here EXPIRING!

And they'll pass me by not noticing everything I've done, everything I am right now, everything that, from this moment on, will be less and less good as my life expires and I start to die without her, without ever getting to show her that I, at one point, was great! That I am, right now, before the fibers of my jeans begin to loosen and the veins recess back into my emaciated arms, great! That I am, now and only now, great! And for what?!

What's the point of going to my aunt's house? What's the point of living in Queens? I hate Queens! It's nowhere near anything! I have to take three fucking subways just to get to the fucking subway! I hate doing push-ups! I hate basketball! And I hate my dumb cultural anthropologist friend – all he ever talks about is Samoa! I am at my goddamn peak and no one is even looking! LOOK AT ME! LOOK AT ME! You non-entities! You stupid morons! You imbeciles! You blind moron tourist imbeciles! Where the hell is she!?! This is so ridiculous!!! Where the hell is she? I'm getting furious!!! I am in my jeans!!! I AM IN MY JEANS!!!

Okay, relax. Calm down. Stay positive. You have no idea what her life is like. You have no idea what she's doing. She's probably sitting somewhere waiting for me. If anything. *She's* probably waiting for *me*. That's the irony of it all, right? That's the irony of life, right? The cruel irony of my life.

No, I'm sure she'll be here any minute.

Yeah.

I'm pretty sure Jerry said this weekend. Although, next weekend is Easter, I think, so maybe that's what he meant. Maybe it's next weekend, I never actually celebrated Easter. No. No, I'm pretty sure it was this weekend. I should give him a call.

Or I could just give it another few minutes. That's probably the best thing to do. Just give it another minute or two. And then I'll head home.

Yeah, just another minute.

A BULLY DOES HIS RESEARCH

Well well well, if it isn't little Tommy. Gimme your lunch money, dweeb! Hand it over! What? Are you scared? Are you worried about your family's financial situation now that your parents are separated? Well, boo-hoo-hoo! You probably think it's your fault, don't you? And even though your mommy told you that it had nothing to do with you, that you didn't make Daddy fall in love with his hygienist and run away to that ashram in Oregon, it still feels unsettling. You lie awake telling yourself, "If I had just loved them more, if I had just gotten better grades or was nicer to Grandma when she was in the hospital after her stroke in November, they would still be together." And now you have to give me the money your mother gives you every morning because she can't pack a bag lunch since her insomnia and reliance on Ambien makes her too groggy. Well, cry me a river!

Well well well, if it isn't Mr. Sellowitz, the science teacher, catching me in the act of stealing little Tommy's lunch money. Well, *Smell*owitz, smell this: I'm not Claude Monet! Yeah, that's right. I know you're threatened by me, but unconsciously associating me with Monet's not gonna help. Yeah, I know you wanted to go to RISD since you were my age but you couldn't get in and now you're stuck teaching sixth grade science. Well, boo-hoo-hoo! You probably thought you were the future of impressionistic painting, doing your high school art project on a postmodern take on Monet's *Water Lilies*, with real lilies mounted in a 3-D diorama inside a tank of water. Well, guess what? It wasn't good enough for RISD and it's certainly not good enough for your stepfather, Aaron Segura, the beloved art critic who never liked your work to begin with. Sorry, teach!

Well well well, if it isn't Principal O'Malley, here to suspend me for stealing little Tommy's lunch money and talking back to Mr. Sellowitz. I bet it feels good punishing me, right? Lording your limited power over an adolescent bully? Makes you feel big and strong, doesn't it? Especially since I have such a nice head of hair and you started experiencing rapid male pattern baldness when you were only sixteen years old. Well, boo-hoo-hoo! You tried everything, didn't you? First the natural remedies because you were too embarrassed to tell your doctor that you were going bald and couldn't afford a prescription for anything that would actually work. So you tried eating sardines every day for a year in the faint hope that it would help. And then, by the time you could afford Propecia, it was too late because your hairline had already receded and Propecia has little success of actually regrowing hair shafts from dead follicles, especially in the temple lobe region, where you were most explicitly affected. Suck it!

Well well well, if it isn't my father, here to pick me up from school after I was suspended for stealing little Tommy's lunch money, talking back to Mr. Sellowitz, and showing Principal O'Malley that his need for power is rooted in unresolved trauma relating to his early male pattern baldness. Thanks for the ride home, Pops! Is it weird to pick me up in the middle of the day or does it highlight the fact that Mom's the one with the real job? Does it reconfirm, in some unconscious or even conscious way, that you've lost all sense of pride and masculinity? Did it initially seem interesting to have Mom keep her job at the law firm while you stay home to raise the kids? Did you brag to your friends that you were proud to be eschewing gender norms? Well, boo-hoo-hoo! I bet you feel a burning sense to go out into the world and get even the most menial job just to feel like a person again, once you realized the novel you thought you'd write with your new free time wasn't ever going to materialize and you'd be stuck walking around the house in dirty sweatpants, looking at the clock and waiting for the woman you used to know to come back with the bacon. Psych!

Well well well, if it isn't the town bully, grounded in his bedroom, looking in the mirror and questioning his behavior after stealing little Tommy's lunch money, talking back to Mr. Sellowitz, revealing Principal O'Malley's inner demons, and emasculating his father. So, has it really come to this? A cliched moment of self-reflection from the hardened aggressor? Well, boo-hoo-hoo! You probably think that endlessly harassing people with your well-detailed and overly analytical personal criticisms will make you feel better? You probably think you can keep everyone at a safe emotional distance if you put everyone down? You probably think that, if no one can get close to you and you remain hardened against the world, you'll never get hurt? That if no one likes you, you could remain a safe little bubble?! Bite me!

VIII.
LANGUAGE

NICK GARRETT'S REVIEW OF RACHEL LOWENSTEIN'S NEW BOOK, GETTING AWAY

Cara Dawson, the hapless heroine of the "must-read" novel *Getting Away*, proclaims, "The world and all its people love me!"

One assumes that Rachel Lowenstein, Miss Dawson's creator, must share the feeling. The literary world has been taken by storm with its new darling-of-the-moment, the auspicious twenty-six-year-old Lowenstein, and though the excitement seems only to be building, one gets the wary sense Miss Lowenstein's literary prospects seem gloomy at best.

Lowenstein has been praised for her tragicomic treatise on one woman's journey from hopeless romantic to empowered, staunchly single woman, and book clubs around the country have taken up Lowenstein's "authentic" criticism of the male gaze as their new cause célèbre.

But where does all this vitriol stem from? Lowenstein has stated in interviews that her awful experiences with one particularly "narcissistic" man drove her to write this bestseller, which she says "proves that women don't need love to feel happy." Although one wonders what Lowenstein did to this "mystery man" to make him so "narcissistic." After all, it takes two to tango, Miss Lowenstein, two to tango.

Like Ayn Rand before her, Lowenstein uses a "plot" merely as a vehicle to deliver her dogmatism: in this case, an attack on one seemingly harmless man.

Lowenstein's story begins fourteen years ago as readers are introduced to Cara, a scrawny seventh grader in the Philadelphia suburbs. Though a loner, she is starry-eyed, quixotically pursuing unrequited love after unrequited love, in search for what Cara calls her "sole soul mate."

A late bloomer, Cara goes through high school without ever kissing a boy, something that Miss Lowenstein has joked about in interviews as being "unfortunately based in truth." At college she meets a young man named Mick Barrett in an elevator and later tells her roommate, "Tonight, I met my sole soul mate."

Cara's premature declaration of love initially seems sweet, but her expectations for Barrett are clearly too high. Does Cara consider that placing the burden of "sole soul mate" on a nineteen-year-old college sophomore is possibly more than Barrett can handle? And, considering the pressures put on Barrett by his recently divorced parents (a detail Miss Lowenstein predictably glosses over), perhaps Barrett is not in a place to settle down with a wife and kids, something Cara conveniently never seems to consider.

Is it only this humble critic who finds Mick Barrett to be the lone sympathetic figure of *Getting Away*?

Cara and Barrett begin dating and, though their relationship seems stable, a more thorough retrospective reveals cracks in the otherwise polished veneer. For example, the young couple graduates college, Cara with a BFA in Creative Writing and Barrett with the more "sensible" economics degree that Cara encouraged him to pursue despite his inclinations toward painting. "There should only be one artist in the family," Cara probably said in a scene presumably cut from the book. "I need a man who can support my writing and our children," Cara most likely continued, bluntly crushing any dreams Barrett might have had for a life in the arts.

The couple moves to Westchester (though insightful readers will get the sense that Barrett would have preferred to spend a few years in the city) in order for Cara to have her precious "quietude" for writing her precious novels, a goal that readers are somehow asked to find noble because it's creatively "pure," as though creativity is somehow on moral par with curing cancer. And Barrett is forced to work for an Internet advertising agency in Southern Westchester, a neighborhood that Lowenstein mischaracterizes as "diverse" because, were Cara to ever actually visit Barrett at his office, she would have realized that working two blocks from the South Bronx is terrifying and that "diversity" is a euphemism that only a pampered writer like Lowenstein would use to describe the experience of almost getting mauled by myriad cultures from the world's great diasporas on a daily basis.

Lowenstein continues to demonize Barrett, in such an

unbelievably manipulative way that readers who have never met a Machiavellian woman like Lowenstein or Cara would think she was writing the screenplay for the Mussolini biopic.

Consider the section where Cara wants to spend the day toiling away on her Great American Novel and then attend her mother's birthday dinner. In the morning, she asks Barrett if he could stop by the dry cleaners on his way home from work to pick up her red blouse so that she can wear it to the dinner. Barrett agrees because, frankly, what the hell else is he going to do now that his life has become a dreamless landscape of chores?

So Cara gets to work, writing in the study she never allows Barrett access to (*quelle surprise!*), and when Barrett comes home from work, he is empty-handed. Lowenstein has Barrett mutter something about the dry cleaners being "closed," but clearly readers are supposed to pity the blouse-less Cara in a way usually reserved for the terminally ill.

However, Lowenstein neglects to report that the dry cleaners in question closes promptly at 7:00 and the last express train is at 6:36, so Barrett either has to catch the 5:48, which stops in Larchmont, or catch the 6:36 and literally sprint to the dry cleaners in his suit and after working a full day. Cara is a writer with no set schedule, but Barrett is the one responsible for picking up the clothes? Once again, readers are treated to yet another distorted image of the put-upon Cara and the negligent Barrett.

The next section, which details Barrett and Cara's reconciliation and sexual rejuvenation, is filled with surprisingly beautiful prose, showing Lowenstein's great gift for description when truly moved by her subject matter. She artfully describes Barrett's face while he sleeps: "The moon shone down on his soft features and Cara had the urge to slow down time so she could stare at him forever."

And Lowenstein really finds her linguistic footing when writing about the couple's passionate lovemaking: "Barrett's thrusts were explorations, colonizing her undiscovered body, taking her virginal copper and sending shivers down her golden spine."

It is these hopeful passages that make readers feel like Lowenstein may have a real future—and that she may do the sensible thing and come back to Barrett. Or whomever Barrett is based on.

But just as quickly as Lowenstein introduces us to this lusciousness, she sheathes it as *Getting Away* returns to its customarily vindictive (and hackneyed) prose.

She begins to detail the couple's inevitable demise in a way that feels, in this critic's opinion, deliriously one-sided. Like when Barrett tells Cara that he does not want her mother to stay over at their house for the weekend and she calls Barrett "abusive." When Barrett asks how that simple request constitutes "abuse," Cara storms out of the house. What Lowenstein seems to "conveniently" leave out of the narrative is that Cara's mother is the most demanding, infuriating, overbearing, and manipulative woman on the Eastern Seaboard (although one should not be surprised to discover this after reading two hundred pages of the angry faux-feminist diatribe that is her progeny's *Getting Away*). One time, Barrett drove forty-five miles in a blizzard to pick up Cara's mother, who refused to take the bus because "it smelled funny."

And the chapter where Cara finally asks for a divorce, which reads like Lowenstein's pièce de résistance, is a groveling and pathetic cry for sympathy even though she knows that what she did was wrong: not just that she left Barrett, but the *way* she left Barrett. To change the locks while he was at work that day was just so punishing. It just made him feel so small and so stupid. He wasn't even angry. He just felt alone.

And they had good times. They really did. It's probably hard for Cara to remember how much they felt for each other because she's so clouded with inexplicable rage, but they really loved each other. And Barrett would do almost anything to just have one good day back with Cara.

And I guess Barrett hopes that maybe somewhere Cara is reading this. Maybe in that café they used to go to on Peterson with the hookah bar or at that park where they used to make out under the vandalized statue of the horse. And maybe, if Cara wants, they could meet there again sometime. Not to date or anything, but just to talk. Just to clear the air. Just so he can tell her that he's really proud of what she's doing and that she deserves the great success she's having and that he always knew she would do great things.

He just wants to look into her eyes and tell her that he loves her. He just wants to feel her soft palm in his and stroke the inside of her fingers one last time. Despite everything, he still loves her. And he always will.

ONE AND A HALF STARS.

A SHORT STORY WRITTEN WITH THOUGHT-TO-TEXT TECHNOLOGY

It was a Thursday but it felt like a Monday to John. And John loved Mondays. He thrived at work. He dismissed the old cliché of dreading Monday mornings and refused to engage in watercooler complaints about "the grind" and empty conversations that included the familiar back-and-forth: "How was your weekend?" "Too short!" Yes, John liked his work and was unashamed.

I should probably get another latte. I've just been sitting here with this empty cup. But then I'll start to get jittery. I'll get a decaf. No, that's stupid, it feels stupid to pay for a decaf. I can't justify that.

John was always impatient on the weekends; he missed the formal structure of the business week. When he was younger he used to stay late after school on Fridays and come in early on Mondays, a pattern his mother referred to with equal parts admiration and disdain as "studying overtime."

Jesus, I've written another loser.

Now, John spent his weekends doing yard work at the Tudor house Rebecca left him after their divorce. Rebecca, with her almond eyes—both in shape and color—could never be his enemy.

That barista keeps looking at me. She'll probably ask me to leave if I don't buy something. She's kind of attractive. Not her hair—her hair seems stringy—but her face is nice. I should really buy something.

Their divorce was remarkably amicable. In fact, John would often tell his parents, "Rebecca and I are better friends now than when we were married!" Moreover, John looked forward to the day when he and Rebecca, with their new partners, would reminisce about their marriage, seeing it in a positive light like two mature adults.

Maybe I'll just get a pumpkin spice loaf. That way I can still sit here without going through a whole production of buying a coffee and giving my name and feeling like an asshole while it gets made.

But if John was being honest, the house did get lonely on the weekends. Rebecca's parents had been generous enough to leave John the house even though they had paid for it. John was still struggling to get his short story writing—I mean, his *painting*—career off the ground, and Rebecca and her family had been more than supportive, even during the breakup.

Maybe the barista's looking at me because she thinks I'm attractive. I am in my blue shirt. So she has stringy hair. Who am I to complain about stringy hair? Who do I think I am? Cary Grant?

And now John was doing temp work at the law firm of Fleurstein & Kaplowitz to get himself righted again. He had a strong six-month plan: he would save some money to pay Rebecca's parents back for the house and be able to take some time off to focus on his writing—*on his painting.* In a few months, he would be back on his feet, probably even engaged to someone new. Maybe even that barista. Yes, almost paradoxically, temp work provided John with the stability he craved.

This is shit. It is utter shit.

Actually, in moments of great self-reflection, John hated his work. Who was he kidding? He was doing temp work. No one has ever liked temp work. It reinforced his feeling of instability, confirmed his cynical view of the job market, and took him away from the only thing he ever enjoyed doing, which was writing short stories—I mean *painting! Painting!* John enjoyed *painting!*

I think I have to pee.

And John was a great painter.

Literally every single person on line for the bathroom looks homeless. Maybe I can just go in and not touch anything. I'll just lift the seat up with my shoe.

John often wondered how Steve Bowman from college was having so much success while John was stuck doing temp work in a futile attempt to pay Rebecca's passive-aggressive parents back for a house he didn't even want them to buy. And Steve Bowman was a talentless hack who even admitted to

John that he only writes—*paints!*—so he can "bag women." He actually said "bag women." But Rebecca thinks he's "interesting" and that they could "have a real life together." I hope they both die of cancer. What did John have with Rebecca? How was that not "real"? Maybe if Rebecca's parents had let John breathe instead of forcing their hypocritical Christian "values" down his throat every chance they got, their relationship would have been more "real." Good luck, Steve Bowman. I hope you like having a mother-in-law with no boundaries.

I think I will get another latte. That barista is so sexy. I'd love to pull her stringy hair while we have sex on my floor.

John would often go to Rebecca and Steve's new house in the middle of the night and just stare in their window.

She probably has a back tattoo. So slutty.

John would secretly hope to see Steve and Rebecca fighting. He would fantasize about seeing their silhouettes through the window, Rebecca throwing the telephone at Steve and him ducking but it still hitting him in the head. John would get aroused by this fantasy.

I'll say something cool like, "The coffee's not the only thing hot in here." And she'll probably be like, "I get off at seven." And I'll probably say something like, "I don't have a real job, so any time's good for me." Jesus, who am I kidding? I'm a loser. She would never like me. Even a stringy-haired barista with a slutty back tattoo would never like me.

But of course John never saw anything in Steve and Rebecca's window. He thought of urinating in a glass bottle and throwing it through their window, but he couldn't even work up the courage to do that. He was a loser who couldn't even commit a petty act of vandalism. He was a dumb dumb stupid dumb writer—*painter!*—who couldn't even afford an office, so he wrote—*painted!*—in a Starbucks because he got fired from Fleurstein & Kaplowitz for making copies of his stories—*paintings!*—when he was supposed to be copying legal briefs for those corrupt corporate shylocks. And Rebecca would never come back to him and no one would ever love him and he was going to die fat and bald and alone and miserable in the ugly house his in-laws bought to suffocate and kill him!

Maybe I'll get a tea. I like that hibiscus one. It's sweet but not too sweet. It's nice. It's a nice flavor.

And maybe I will get a slice of that pumpkin loaf. I think I had it before. I think I definitely liked it. I think it must be seasonal. I haven't seen it in a while.

I'll eat and drink and then get back to work. Everything seems to be flowing well. It was a little tough getting into it but now it's really flowing. It's weird how I do that—how I think I can't write something and suddenly I'm carried away and then I can't stop writing. I think I'm too hard on myself. I think I punish myself for no reason. But I think I'm really hitting my stride now. I'll just get that tea. That nice hibiscus tea.

And then get back to work.

IF I WAS FLUENT IN . . .

French

FRENCHMAN IN TRAIN COMPARTMENT: Wow, this American guy looks so stupid.

SECOND FRENCHMAN IN TRAIN COMPARTMENT: Yes, American guys are all stupid, both in their looks and their brains.

FRENCHMAN: Luckily he can't understand what we're saying because, most likely, he only speaks English.

SECOND FRENCHMAN: That is definitely a safe assumption to make about him.

FRENCHMAN: Yes, Americans can only speak English. That is something that I know for sure. It is a fact.

SECOND FRENCHMAN: Let's continue to insult him in front of his dumb American face.

FRENCHMAN: Yes, it is so much fun because it feels at once safe, because he doesn't speak French, and dangerous, because of his close proximity.

ME: Actually, I speak French fluently and I understand what you are saying about me.

SECOND FRENCHMAN: (*blushing*) Oh, goodness.

ME: And although you think you are insulting me, it is you who will ultimately feel the burden of shame as your condescending assumptions and misguided linguistic pride will prove to be a stain on you and your nation.

FRENCHMAN: He is right. I feel embarrassed now.

SECOND FRENCHMAN: Yes, he showed us, personally, and France, at large, to be both arrogant and foolish.

Hindi

WAITER AT INDIAN RESTAURANT: Hello, sir, welcome to an authentic Indian restaurant. Do you have any questions about the menu?

ME: Yes. Why does all of your food always make me sick?

WAITER: Because we serve our American customers the kind with the weird spices that gives them diarrhea.

ME: Oh.

WAITER: Yes, it's official policy at all Indian restaurants.

ME: Well, what do you serve your Indian patrons?

WAITER: We give them a better kind of Indian food, which does not cause diarrhea.

ME: Can you give me the better kind?

WAITER: Yes, of course. Since you asked in my language, I feel more comfortable accommodating you.

ME: Thank you.

WAITER: Please don't tell your American friends about the option to get Indian food that does not give them diarrhea.

ME: Of course I won't tell them. It'll be our little secret.

Portuguese

BRAZILIAN GANGSTER: Hey, American tourist! I am going to kidnap you and hold you for political and financial ransom.

ME: No, please don't do that.

GANGSTER: Wait a second. You speak Portuguese?

ME: Yes, I do. I am fluent.

GANGSTER: Wow. Where did you study it?

ME: At a school in New York that mostly caters to diplomats and other internationally aware individuals.

GANGSTER: You mean the Learning Annex?

ME: That's right.

GANGSTER: The one on 103rd Street?

ME: Yes. How do you know about that branch?

GANGSTER: It's one of the most popular places on the Upper West Side to learn my language. It would be embarrassing if I did not know it.

ME: Good point.

GANGSTER: I don't live in a bubble, you know.

ME: Of course not. My apologies. Are you still going to kidnap me?

GANGSTER: No, you are now a friend and are therefore free
to go.

ME: It was nice to meet you.

GANGSTER: The pleasure was all mine. Good luck with your
studies.

ME: And you, your war.

Aramaic

JESUS CHRIST: Excuse me, heathen.

ME: Jesus? What are You doing in New York? Are You here for
the Second Coming?

JESUS: No, I just wanted to try that new Shake Shack place everyone's talking about.

ME: Oh, yeah. Their burgers are pretty decent.

JESUS: I heard the line is usually insane though.

ME: It's long, but it moves.

JESUS: Do you think you could come and wait on line with
Me? I'm kind of lonely.

ME: *You're* lonely? I would have assumed You'd have like a bil-
lion friends.

JESUS: Yeah, Me too! But no one here understands Aramaic
except this one theology professor at Columbia who's
kind of creepy. He kept asking Me these totally personal
questions about My mom.

ME: Weird.

JESUS: I know! I was like, *"Stalker!"* And then he wanted to
know if the Shroud of Turin was real and I was like,

"Mind your own business."

ME: I don't even know what the Shroud of Turin is.

JESUS: Which is why it's so *refreshing* to hang out with you! Hey, would you be into being My new friend?

ME: Yeah, I'd be down for that. My friend Jeff just moved to Boulder for grad school so I kind of have a slot open.

JESUS: Awesome. And since We're cool now, you are guaranteed a special place in Heaven.

ME: Really? Even if I do something bad in life?

JESUS: Yup. Since you speak My language, you will always be able to get into Heaven.

MY SPAM PLAYS HARD TO GET

To: Me
From: Alexxxa
Subject: Miss you babe!

Hey babe,
Where are you? I miss chatting with you! I've just been sitting here alone on my webcam, naked, waiting for you.

In fact, I've been waiting so long I took up embroidery, which has been amazing! It's both meditative *and* creative. And I'm about to finish my first sweater! So if you sign on, I may be deep inside a blanket stitch. Sorry if I have to keep you waiting, honey!

I've gotten really hot just thinking about you!

So, to cool down, I started rereading Chaucer! Wow! What a rediscovery! So dense. But so (deceptively) fun! Can't wait to see you, sweetie! But if you sign on tonight, I might be busy traversing Canterbury!

If I *am* busy, you should go chat with one of my girl-friends, like Trixxxie or Roxxxana. They're great! Of course, I'd love to get dirty with you, but I totally understand if you want to hang with some new chicks. I'm actually not so into the idea of a monogamous webcam relationship anyway. I have big dreams! I want to flirt with perverts from Paris! And even Africa! Maybe learn to play an instrument, besides my usual ones!

So call me!

Or don't!

Either way.

<3 Alexxxa <3

To: Me
From: Mr. Jeffrey Obassanjo
Subject: Urgent Reply Needed

Dear Sir or Madam,

It is with a heavy heart that I inform you of the death of my uncle, a rich Nigerian prince. After his passing, we discovered that he had acquired a significant sum of 48 MILLION US DOLLARS.

Unfortunately, for this money to be released, it must be transferred to a United States bank account.

In exchange for access to a US account, we would be happy to reward the recipient with 10 percent of this sum (4.8 MILLION US DOLLARS).

We have selected YOU as the recipient.

However, we are also considering your neighbor Larry Stanowitz. We know you think Larry already has enough money, constantly flaunting his new Peugeot and grocery bags from Balducci's, but we're not looking to do charity. Just for a bank account.

If Larry is unable to accept the money, we're also considering your colleague Sheila Drucker. Even though she's a corporate brownnoser and your only direct competition for the VP promotion, we think she might be a good candidate for this financial gift. Again, we're not looking for a model citizen. Just a bank account.

Please respond to us at your earliest convenience.

But if you don't, as mentioned, we will likely just go to Larry or Sheila. They seem pretty cool too.

Sincerely,
Mr. Obassanjo

To: Me
From: GmailAlertz
Subject: Confirm GMail Password!

Dear Account Member,

Your Gmail account requires you to confirm your password. If you do not reply to this email with your password within twenty-four hours, your email account may be blocked.

Which might not be such a bad thing.

I mean, do you really need to check your email so frequently? Your incessant monitoring has become a kind of psychosis. It's eroded your relationships and deactivated your slower, but more substantive, critical-thinking skills.

This love affair with communication has become an addiction, a fixation for which society at large—not just you—is both the victim and the aggressor. Whether it's the constant bombardment from your mother with the pictures from her book club (it's called a book club, not a take-a-picture-of-everything-you-eat-during-book-club club) or passive-aggressive "updates" from your friends with children, telling you how happy they are and how parenting is so much easier than they expected, it's all a dragon you will always chase and never catch.

Your Gmail account is just another prison of your own making, a panopticon of desperation surrounding you with guards of loneliness.

So you could respond to this email with your

password, but it'll probably just perpetuate this dangerous cycle.

Maybe it's best if you lay low for a bit. Enjoy the out-
doors. Go for a walk. Talk to a stranger.

Sorry to bother you.

Gmail

MANAGEABLE TONGUE TWISTERS

Peter Johnson selected a group of jarred spices.
If Peter Johnson selected a group of jarred spices,
How many jarred spices did Peter Johnson select?

How much lumber could a woodchuck discard
If a woodchuck could discard lumber?

Sally peddles fish exoskeletons down by the beach.

Fuzzy Wuzzy had been a bear.
But he was bald.
So, if this was the case,
He couldn't have been very fuzzy, right?

Moses thinks his phalanges are perennials.
But Moses is wrong.
For no one's phalanges are perennials,
Like Moses thinks his phalanges are.

One smart fellow,
He thought he was deserving of this title.
Two smart fellows,
They also thought they were deserving of this title.
Three smart fellows,
They all thought they were deserving of this collective
designation.

Red-and-yellow leather.
Red-and-yellow leather.
(")

New York is different.

Elizabeth Botter paid money for margarine.
But the margarine
For which Elizabeth Botter paid was tart.
So Elizabeth Botter paid money for some superior
margarine,
And it made Elizabeth Botter's
Once-tart mixture good.

My mother coerced me to destroy my Mars-brand chocolate
candies.

James bifurcated corn,
Although I don't really give a shit.

I scream.
Then you join me.
Pretty soon we all find ourselves
Shouting praises for frozen custard.

IX.
WE ONLY
HAVE TIME
FOR ONE
MORE . . .

WE ONLY HAVE TIME
FOR ONE MORE

Thanks a lot! You guys have been a great audience! Buffalo is truly one of my favorite cities. We love coming through here and stopping at the best music venue in town, the Rotting Tree! Unfortunately, we only have time for one more song.

I wish we could stay here rocking and rolling with you guys all night, but for a variety of reasons, we only have time for one more.

Our bassist Steve Barron's got two kids so he can't stay out too late. I know what you're thinking: "Steve has two kids? Last year when you guys played the Tree, he didn't have any." Well, he had twins. First time out of the gate and he winds up with two. If that isn't a real baptism by fire . . . go figure. The man is fertile.

And Mark Platt, our fiddle player, has a blister on his

thumb the size of—I kid you not—a small golf ball. Every note he plays is a kind of hell for him. So that's another reason we can only play one more song.

Dan Simmons, our drummer, actually doesn't know any more of our songs. Sammy Marber, our previous drummer, left the band due to "creative differences" (a.k.a. he's an ego-maniacal psychopath with a coke problem) and Dan hasn't bothered to learn the whole oeuvre. So if we played any more songs, it would basically be without drums.

As for me, I wish we could play all night. I got nothing else going on. I kind of gave up my life for the band. I write the songs, I'm the lead singer, and the band is named "Peter Ja-worski and His Band" and I'm Peter Jaworski. I've really strug-gled to create a full life and it gets lonely, if I'm being honest. I go home to no one. I eat TV dinners. Lots of Netflix. It's not glamorous. And my life has become so narrow that I don't re-ally have any new experiences to write about. That's why you guys heard three songs about how fast my Honda Accord is. The first two were kind of interesting, but that last one was hackneyed. I get it.

Anyway, we also only have time for one more because Jojo, our mixer, has a gambling problem and apparently has to Skype with her bookie. The whole thing seems irresponsible, but the truth is, she's pretty good at mixing the music and we really don't pay enough to get anybody better.

Then there's the whole issue of the unions. Listen, I'm as pro-union as the next guy. My parents were teachers. But if we go a minute past eleven, everyone goes to time and a half and I get docked.

And Pinkie on tambourine actually has a date. Can you believe that? Look at him: he's got that patchy beard and he's like five-foot-nothing, but for whatever reason women seem to like him.

I'm also getting the sense that some of the roadies don't love Peter Jaworski and His Band the same way I love Peter Jaworski and His Band. I asked Dwayne Beemer if he liked a lyric I was tooling around with last week—"Your love is like sandpaper in my veins"—and he looked at me like I was the dumbest person in the world. And now I have his judgy face emblazoned in my mind when we play "Sandpaper Blood." I understand he may be a little disgruntled—he does carry the amps for a third-tier emo-grunge band in the Lower Great Lakes region—but he could show a little more tact. I have feelings too, Dwayne Beemer.

We also only have time for one more because Teddy Faour has reservations at the Chophouse, Aliya Coleman bought a Wi-Fi pass that expires at midnight, Shepherd Brennan needs to wash his hair, and Rory Thompson has GERD.

These are just some of the reasons that we only have time for one more.

So without further ado, our final song. Ladies and gentlemen: "Matte Black Honda"!

ACKNOWLEDGMENTS

Thank you to my wonderful editors Peter Blackstock at Grove, Susan Morrison at the *New Yorker*, and Chris Monks at *McSweeney's* for encouraging me to value (respectively): brevity, maturity, and not making every story about a nine-year-old boy harrowing. Thank you also to Judy Hottensen, Deb Seager, and Morgan Entrekin at Grove, David Remnick and Emma Allen at the *New Yorker* and Dave Eggers at *McSweeney's* for your extraordinary institutions and the honor of being included. Thank you to my tireless agents Simon Green, Michael Kives, Craig Gering, and Olivier Sultan, who ensure that more than just the people on this page read the stories on the other pages. Thank you to Jean Jullien, who is funnier without words than most are with. Thank you also to Lee Gabay, Jim Beggarly, Anna Strout, Gabe Millman, Brian Westmoreland, and Mia Wasikowska. Finally, thank you to my supportive family, who never seem to exercise their veto power even when the joke's on them.